Windows on the World

Tales from a Suffolk Village Bed and Breakfast

Fiona Denny

To my uncle, John Talbot Glover

1930 - 2015

It is an idle question to ask whether he will be remembered a century hence. If his name was forgotten immediately after his death it would only be like cutting down an oak after its acorns have sewn a forest.

Adapted from George Eliot (1819 – 1880) on the influence of Thomas Carlyle

Windows on the World

Tales from a Suffolk Village Bed & Breakfast

Chapter One: The Arrival

It was only after they put in new windows that I realised this could be a long term relationship.

After all, the Diocese would never have paid for new windows. This was definitely a fresh chapter. I'd been in slumber since the old vicar passed away. Occasionally a door would slam and voices echo round the empty rooms but nothing much happened. I watched the wild roses and brambles grow; their long arms reaching upwards and outwards strangling the ash and oak, smothering the honeysuckle and hiding the fence panels. Nothing happened for months and then months stretched into years.

I took notice of Art and Diana from the beginning. They leaned over the gate chattering excitedly, walked up the drive, peered through the windows and tramped round the garden. They came back twice. They talked about a vegetable patch. I heard the word "chickens" and I thought to myself: "Hey ho, are these my new tenants?"

There had been other viewers, a mixture of families and developers. This was the third time I had been put up for sale and there was always a lot of interest. But each time something seemed to go wrong and the sale collapsed.

Art and Diana spent Christmas here before moving in. They put a little tree on a table and huddled in sleeping bags on the floor. They bought their cat, Mr Mistoffelees, (MM for short). It was freezing. The single glazed Crittall windows kept out the wind but the frost seeped into the room. After Christmas they disappeared, driven out by the cold, and that's when I got some new windows.

Art and Diana didn't have children, just MM, who attacked my trees with her sharp claws. What they did have was energy and gradually I was transformed. It was a long

6

slow process but after two years our Bed and Breakfast was ready to open.

But before I share my tales of those that came to stay, let me say something about my new tenants. Humans use the term 'owners' but, as far as we houses are concerned, you are all tenants. We will be here long after you have gone.

They were very different characters. Diana was like a whirlwind, full of ideas and plans. She was in her early forties, medium height and build with short, cropped, dark hair beginning to grey at the edges. She worked full time in Norwich so she was out early and home late.

Art was a few years older and took life at a more sedentary pace. He was lean (tending to skinny in my view) and clean shaven. He had Multiple Sclerosis and soon after moving to Minefield, he stopped work. Our bed and breakfast project was his idea.

By the time I was built in the 1970s, the 5-acre field I stood in had been broken up into smaller parcels. Diana and Art worked hard to track down the owners and put the pieces back together. The purchase of Ash Meadow completed the jigsaw.

Ash Meadow came with its own unexploded bomb, dropped from a German airplane in World War II. For decades it lay silent, covered with the brick rubble from a neighbouring bombed house. Art whipped up the interest of some World War II enthusiasts who arrived with a metal detector. I'd always enjoyed Last of the Summer Wine and they reminded me of Compo, Clegg and Foggy as they pogo-ed down the meadow and on to the UXB site. They were there for hours and left empty handed, enthusiasm unabated.

Minefield was the name of our village. It was a pretty little place – a hamlet almost - in the middle of nowhere. You passed by it en route to somewhere else. It was this anonymity which preserved its character. A medieval church, a medley of creaking and topsy-turvy cottages filled the high street. Those new to the village were determined to preserve this rural idyll and re-energise its sense of community.

Over time the village shop and three of the four public houses that once lined the main road had closed. The newcomers joined forces with the locals: mounted a campaign, raised funds and bought the surviving hostelry, The Poacher, which they staffed with volunteers and ran as a combined pub, shop and bakery. They turned the telephone kiosk into a library and ran a farmers' market each month from the village hall.

Many of these villagers will weave in and out of our story so it feels right to introduce them now.

Step forward Charles Bowman. Our openly gay, extremely camp and very exacting parish clerk. He was also a church activist, lay preacher and self-appointed guardian of our beautiful medieval church. The prayer books were counted in and out and the church cleaning rota was prioritised above all things. Family bereavement, graduations, ill health were all of less importance than the church cleaning rota.

It was the new vicar I felt most sorry for. The Reverend Sarah Long was appointed to replace 3 vicars and a rector. She covered 8 parishes single handed and, to save money, was accommodated in a new bungalow. It was her arrival that had caused my redundancy. I didn't hold it against her.

Life would have been difficult for the most organised person. But Rev Sarah wasn't organised. She had a *'heart of gold'* instead (which was a polite way of saying she was scatty}. She constantly found herself at loggerheads with Charles. He disliked her on principle because she was a woman. After all, he'd only just got over the church's defection from the 1662 Book of Common Prayer.

The irony of a gay lay preacher challenging the propriety of female vicars was not lost on anyone except Charles but somehow no one ever mentioned it. Except Joe of course. But then Joe was at the edge of social circles and didn't come inside them. He introduced himself as a gardener. It was difficult to pinpoint what gardens he did work in. He was amazingly fit and strong despite his small frame but his leathery, lined and weather-beaten face suggested great age. He could have been anywhere between fifty and eighty. He spent much time walking around the village with his dog 'Munch', regularly carrying gardening tools to the allotment or wheeling barrows back home and was forever ready with his opinion and advice.

It was said that if you wanted a rumour spreading quickly you should tell Joe. If you told him in the morning, a version of the story would be where you needed it to be by the following evening.

In the beginning, Diana was completely spooked by Joe. It seemed as if every time she appeared outdoors there he was. "Morning" would cry a disembodied voice and into view would come a hand, raised high, and a body (slumped like a turtle).

Sleepy, Christian and middle class. The Suffolk village caricature means something precisely because it captures some kind of truth. Scratch beneath the surface and you soon find that all is not what it seems.

Take the pot smoking Captain for example. Adam Hardy was the talk of the village when he first arrived. He clipped the box hedge surrounding his small cottage and invited the world to take a look on the open garden day. Here was a most respectable man, a wealthy bachelor to boot; a man to invite to dinner parties; to involve in village hall and church affairs and to make up the numbers at bridge. A slim man, moreover. Not unattractive and with an interesting past.

Three years later and Adam's eccentric behaviour (he was something of a recluse), frequent absences and plentiful supplies of cash gave rise to rumours that he was a modern day pirate with a lucrative trade in skippering private vessels (and their smuggled contraband) across the world. This mystery heightened his value. His presence at the dinner table was even more highly sought, especially by the ladies in the parish. As the rumours and stories grew so opinion divided: moral indignation, admiration and even envy.

In most places there is usually an undercurrent of gossip but in Minefield we also had our own anonymous letter writer. Of course everyone knew it was Lucas. He had written rather a lot of letters on a wide range of subjects. Even Art got one:

"Take your eyes off my wife," Lucas wrote, the day after the village hall gardener's quiz. "You have one of your own, *such as she is.*"

Art was mortified until he discovered that he was not alone. Daisy got a letter following her success at the village produce show. Her roses, it was claimed, had been purchased from a local specialist and were not home grown.

Minefielders were, of course, very interested in the comings and goings of other Minefielders. The jungle drums were active but benign. Minefielder idiosyncrasies were known and discussed but not usually condemned outright. They gave life spice and were treated as gifts.

Even the tree warden's constant intrusion into planning law was tolerated. Bert was well known on the parish council for objecting to any building application. He was set on preserving the village and landscape as it was. He was deeply suspicious when Diana and Art bought Ash Meadow. It didn't help that they had bought the land from Bert's childhood sweetheart, Maggie.

Maggie Marsh left the village in the 1960s to pursue free love at Glastonbury. She returned some years later when she inherited her uncle's farm. But it was Bert's older brother she married. Somehow over the years the household became a ménage à trois and this lasted some twenty years until Bert's brother died. Maggie then remarried a retired bank manager and moved to Swaffham leaving Bert abandoned once again.

There is a breed of men whose glass is half empty and whose starting point is to assume the worst. Whether it was natural disposition or his romantic disappointments, Bert could only be described as a grumpy bugger. Given the size of the chip on his shoulder, Bert's position as Tree Warden was entirely apt. Never the most sociable of men, his relationship and subsequent rejection by Maggie, left him more surly and monosyllabic with each passing year.

Now. Let me think. What else do you, dear Reader, need to know before the play begins?

"The Poacher". Our combined village shop/post office/bakery and pub was the heart of our community. Entirely staffed by volunteers it existed on gossip and goodwill. No one minded that food stocks were often out of date or that the volunteers couldn't add up or operate the till. It was a miracle the place existed at all. Its co-ordinator, Jane, was the village's heartbeat. Without her nothing would have been achieved. She managed the shop, press ganged the shop assistants and tried to train them, drove the community bus, led the church choir, chaired the village hall and allotment committees. I was very fond of Jane.

Daisy and Mildred were two Poacher volunteers. Older generation: widow and spinster respectively.

Daisy lived opposite the pub in an idyllic rose-covered cottage. The front garden had a heady mix of meadow flowers that brought swathes of brilliant colour throughout the spring and summer. Just outside the front window was a gnarled pear tree which yielded a fine crop each year.

Daisy still did her stint in The Poacher and, until recently, delivered the Christingle oranges from the boot of her car. She faithfully followed the carol singers up side street and down alley. Most wished she would stop. Her eyes were failing and her car had as many trips to the body shop as it had outings. Her neighbour, Geordie Dave, had fixed her garage door only to have her drive into it twice. The door now hung sorrowfully from one hinge, swinging in the breeze. When the red, rather battered Fiesta was seen careering down the high street Minefielders literally leapt over hedges into nearby gardens.

The end of the line for the Christingles came when she backed into a caroller already unsteady on the ice with an over indulgence of mulled wine and brandy-filled mince pies. The caroller fell over and broke his leg. Next Christmas Minefielders gathered under the village sign and stayed there.

Mildred, by contrast, was ninety-six and sharp as a knife. She was the *'go to'* person for the garden allotment quiz. Smart phones were disallowed after competitors started using "Google". So Mildred's encyclopaedic knowledge was much sought after. Unfortunately, it gave rise to an anti-Mildred faction and a petition to ban the Times National Crossword champion finalist 1971, 72 and 73 from taking part. In the end a handicap of minus 15 points was awarded to the Mildred-bearing team. It made no difference. Year in year out Mildred triumphed.

Mildred did not suffer fools or sentiment. She was sharp and judgemental. This feisty little woman, now crippled by arthritis, could shred grown men with the acidity of her tongue. Formerly the head teacher at Minefield Primary School (long since closed) she had taught many of the current Minefield inhabitants, their parents and grandparents. She had a very long and accurate memory, especially for misdemeanours.

Mildred did have one weakness. It was Geordie Dave. Daisy's neighbour. Fast talking and fast thinking. Dave and his family had moved from Newcastle. No one could quite fathom why. The whole family was quick, street-wise and savvy. They were larger than life in all respects. Taxi driving, antique dealing, luncheon clubs, garden clearance, general maintenance, or acting as unofficial bookmaker – wherever there was a bob to be made Dave, or his wife Kate, could be found. Quite what Mildred and Dave had in common was also a mystery. Perhaps it was his energy and sharp wit. Perhaps he reminded her of someone from her past. We will see ....

And so, the stage is set: the backdrop has been painted and some of the characters introduced. The Minefield Old Vicarage Bed and Breakfast has opened its doors and we await our first customer.

Chapter Two: The Artist

In truth we had to wait a long time but finally the call came.

Sally Brewster booked for 5 days. She sent a lovely little card of a stained glass window confirming the booking. She later told us it was from Gaudi's Sagrada Familia cathedral in Barcelona. Her breakfast demands were very exacting. No dairy and no meat. Diana and Art had spent hours putting together a gut-buster breakfast menu. They now spent days wandering up and down supermarket aisles looking at the labels on packets of food. Everything seemed to contain dairy traces, even bread. Eventually they discovered gluten-free which seemed to deal with the problem albeit at four times the price. Gluten-free bread rolls, soya spread, jam, fruit and soya yoghurt. Yuck.

They were particularly pleased when Sally told them she was attending an art course at a farm just up the road. The artist ran several of these courses a year. This could be the beginning of a steady stream of bookings.

There was only one bed and breakfast room which had been where the vicar met his parishioners. It was a place that resonated with heartache and sorrow. A place where Minefielders had shared the darkest moments of their lives. There were happier times when couples came full of hope and love to prepare for marriage or plan a christening but, in recent times with an aging village population, the room had become more one of death than life.

I was hopeful that this new venture would be just the shot in the arm we all needed. Diana and Art painted my walls a bright yellow. They bought a second-hand wardrobe from one-eyed Bob who kept a furniture emporium in a disused garage in the nearby market town. The vicar's enormous 3 metre bookcase caused a lot of problems. It had been built in situ and was clearly intended to remain inside the room until the house fell down. After strenuous efforts and language, not fit to be repeated, it was man (or woman)-handled outside and taken to the garage. It left a glaring hole in the carpet that was also under siege from moths. Diana and Art had run out of money so they put down some underlay and bought an Indian-patterned burgundy runner. This exotic addition covered up the hole left by the bookcase and was passingly in tune with the newly made burgundy curtains.

There was great excitement and anxiety the day of Sally Brewster's arrival. The moth-eaten carpet was vacuumed and re-vacuumed; the food hygiene certificate and the 5* food hygiene rating were proudly laminated and displayed in a lever arch folder along with a no smoking sign and instructions on what to do if there was a fire.

In the event it was something of an anti-climax. It could hardly have been otherwise. Even a G8 Conference with Heads of State pouring into the house from all directions might not have delivered such was the fever pitch of anticipation.

At 4.30 pm a rather battered white Skoda crunched into the drive. A dishevelled, plump and middle aged woman with blond dyed hair and lots of make up tumbled out. Smiles all round. A formal tour of the room was led by Art with some additional commentary from Diana. Sally's appreciation was noted and welcomed. The counter intuitive and idiosyncratic workings of the shower were explained. Cups of tea offered and accepted. With great bonhomie the three of them sat outside on the patio.

This was our first guest and Diana and Art were keen to make a good impression. They hadn't realised they would lose four hours of their lives in the process. There are some people who tell their life story at the first meeting. Sally was one of them. The first monologue ran on for 45 minutes and was directed at Art. Diana, finding she was superfluous, managed to escape on the pretext of polishing the cat's whiskers. Art was stuck, looking sympathetic and interested by turn and trying not to smile as he caught a glimpse of Diana alternatively hanging herself from an imaginary rope and pulling faces.

Although not unusual, Sally's tale was still one of great sadness. Her first husband had walked out to live with her best friend some ten years ago. She was an anxious woman, lacking in confidence. She had one son, Glen, and was devoted to him although it became clear that the feeling was not reciprocated. She had recently started courting again and her new partner had asked her to move in with him. However Glen was adamantly opposed. He threatened to leave home and never see Sally again if she "*embarrassed him by doing anything so stupid*". As Sally was about to become a grandmother this was not a risk she was prepared to take.

Sally confided that she had recently inherited some money. Glen had asked for the entire amount so that he could buy a house.   Sally had refused and offered to buy him a new car instead. This was regarded as sloppy seconds. Glen was currently sulking and refusing to speak to her. It was the latest stage of a campaign that had involved abuse, sweet talking and threats of physical violence.

"So this course has become a bit of a lifeline you see. Something to look forward to. Claude really is a magnificent artist and a great friend. Without this to hang on to I don't know what I would have done. This is the third year I've done a course with him."

"What kind of art is it?" asked Art.

"Oh very modern, very avant-garde. His methods of teaching are very exacting too. It's a bit like method acting for artists. You have to immerse yourself in the experience. He takes you right back to basics. We spent half the week last time making collages before we were allowed to touch any paint. And you have to use the paint and paper that he recommends. He is such a genius."

Art, who was quite a practical chap, couldn't see anything particularly remarkable in all this.

"That artist is ripping her off," he commented later to Diana as they got ready for bed. "Have you any idea how much he is charging for this week? And then she has to buy her materials through him. It's money for old rope. I wish we'd thought of it!!"

"If he didn't have a reputation then he wouldn't be able to charge. There must be something in it. Whatever else, don't say anything. Even if he is ripping her off. Maybe she needs to believe that something is going right in her life. It's not our business."

"There are lots of things I wish weren't our business," grumbled Art. "Next time don't leave me alone with her. And buy some tissues. I've never had anyone cry within 5 minutes of meeting me. That son of hers sounds no better than the artist. She seems surrounded by crooks."

"Poor baby," said Diana and switched out the light.

"I'm not a social worker you know…"

Early next morning Art wandered into Ash Meadow. He heard a coarse, loud cry coming from the centre of the field.

At first he thought it was their wild pheasant Henry but as his eyes grew accustomed to the bright sunlight he realised it was Sally. She was half naked, waving her arms about and shrieking. I believe you humans call it yoga.

Art stood slightly transfixed not sure whether to make himself known or to bid a hasty retreat.

A disembodied voice floated through the haze.

"Morning." Joe's slouched posture came into view as he trudged down the road with Munch.

Sally turned and waved. On turning back she saw Art staring at her. She blushed coquettishly, picked up her T-shirt and brushed past him.

"She skipped indoors and called me a 'naughty boy'," Art related to Diana as soon as he could find her. "How can I serve her breakfast now? Worst case I'm a voyeur. No scrub that – that's best case. Worst case I'm a new admirer."

Judging by the giggles and flirting over breakfast Sally seemed quite taken with Art. Being a former vicarage this was a new experience for me and I rather enjoyed it. Art was trying to melt into the dining room walls. He escaped whenever possible, only to be called back on the pretext of more gluten free toast or soya milk.

"Your new belle seems in fine spirits this morning," teased Diana.

"Have you let the chickens out yet?" growled Art stomping out to the greenhouse.

Faith, Hope and Charity were the best part of the new look Old Vicarage. They were bantam chickens: two Pekins and a Barbour D'Oucle. Bantams are about a third the size of normal chickens and have feathers on their feet. Art loved them. They would come and sit on his knee and they charged towards him every time he called. They had free roam of the garden and were comical characters that bounced when they moved as if they were on pogo sticks. They spent the day marching round and round the house like little security guards. Scratch and peck, scratch and peck. Charity (the Barbour D'Oucle) had bright orange, black and white speckles. She looked like a little pheasant. Faith and Hope were pure white and lavender respectively. They were a hit with everyone who saw them. The eggs were tiny but tasty. They had an appetite for cake and custard creams which took expression in the colour and flavour of their egg yolk. I loved them too. They were part of the joy of my new life.

Sally left for her course in high spirits. However she was somewhat subdued when she returned at the end of the day and actively sought out Art, her new kindred spirit. She saw through his plain speaking and grumpiness. Art genuinely did care about people, was interested in them and always willing to offer advice. Diana regarded this kindness as something of a double edged sword.

"Listening is usually better than offering advice," she told him. "Especially when you don't know what you are talking about."

However Art seemed to feel it was more important to convey certainty than to worry about detail. So Diana left him to it.

From what I could gather listening to their conversation there were twelve people on the course including Sally.

Eleven were staying together in a large stately house just down the road.

"I asked why I wasn't staying there too. No offence Art but it would have been nice to be together. Claude said there wasn't room. But I booked over nine months ago. They all seem very cliquey. It's just as well I'm only there for the art."

And the next day, she sought Art out again.

"We've now spent two days just cutting out bits of sugar paper to make a collage. I did that last time. This was supposed to be a more advanced course. I know some of these people haven't been here before but even so… And when I try to speak to him he says he will come back to me and then doesn't. He spends all his time with these new people. I didn't have one conversation with him today. I don't know what's happened but I feel I'm being ignored and cut out."

"How much are you paying a day?" asked Art casually.

"The rot's setting in," he later confided to Diana. "The scales are falling from her eyes. I hate it when people are ripped off. Claude Michelle. I ask you. I keep expecting to see a beret and a string of onions. She showed me some pictures of his work. Load of modern rubbish. Red lines and squares."

"Well if you're right, it's a shame," said Diana. "This was something good in her life amongst all that personal rubbish. Now even this turns out to be hollow and false. Where does that leave her? What has she got left?"

"Perhaps I should tell her."

"I wouldn't if I were you. She won't thank you. She needs to find her own way."

If you are keen to help, it's hard to believe that meddling might actually make things worse. Even so I was more with Art than Diana.

Meddling is the business of a vicarage and I truly believe we were a power for good. In the early days my rooms rang with heated ecumenical debates. My vicars and their wives were at the centre of everything that happened in Minefield. Even the rose bushes in my gardens were the talk and envy of everyone for miles around. The children swung from ropes in my trees and made dens in the back wood.

By the time I was put out to grass with my last vicar, Reverend Snow, I was neglected and neglectful. The Reverend had dementia although initially it was well hidden. He was also something of a hoarder. My rooms became more cluttered, dirt-filled and dust ridden and I lost pride in my position. No one came to call. I was redundant well before the Diocese stepped in and sold me. By that time the village had become quite self sufficient with an abundance of lay preachers. Where there is a vacuum something nearly always fills it.

I missed being at the centre of village life and I had never quite lost the conviction that I could be useful again.

So when I saw Sally sobbing before she fell asleep that night, I was reminded of my past life. Not least because her bedroom was where we used to make things right for people. I knew I wasn't a vicarage anymore and that it wasn't our place to intervene. But I felt we ought to do something to help. Perhaps here was a new calling after all.

By the end of Wednesday (Day 3), Sally was very angry. "It's all changed," she told Art. "This isn't like it was before. And I'm clearly a second class citizen. He's asked us to pay another £300 towards materials. I'm not saying he isn't a good artist but it's not like it was on the other courses. He doesn't focus on my – our – development as students. He's out for an easy ride. He just waltzes about the place. That is when he's there at all. Today he disappeared for half the day. And when he is there he's on the phone. I tell you for two pins......"

Her mobile rang. Something of an achievement given the signal quality around here. Art rose to go but Sally put her hand on his arm to stop him leaving.

"Oh ... Hello Glen. Yes I'm on my course. How are you and how is Sylvia? Is the baby OK? Only a few more weeks now...... Yes I don't want to argue either.. I don't think I was unreasonable. I know it's disappointing.... Sorry – the signal is dropping ... You want to know if I've changed my mind? ... No I haven't but I'd still be happy to buy the car for you. Yes I know that you'd like the house but it's a lot of money and to get what you want would use up all my savings. Could you afford the repayments any way? Wouldn't you be better staying with me for the time being? No I'm not trying to trap you. I just want to help. Glen .. Glen just listen to me. I don't deserve that Glen. That's not fair. Yes of course I love you .. you know I do. The baby...? That's not fair. That's blackmail. Glen .... Glen calm down – stop shouting at me Oh Glen please let's just talk about it when I get back..."

The phone went dead.

Sally was visibly shaking. At first she couldn't speak and then the tears started to flow, along with the heavily applied mascara and foundation that gave her courage to face the world.

In jolts and jerks it all came out. But unlike when she first arrived this wasn't a story it was a lived experience and Art came to understand what it felt like to be Sally. The daily verbal attacks. The contempt and disrespect from her son and the feeling that somehow she had created the monster that now lived in her house.

Art was drawn into her world. They started to trade stories of neglect and abuse. Two strangers, both wounded, seeking to heal each other by probing still deeper into those open sores. And yet somehow it made a difference. Perhaps all it takes is the feeling that someone is with you, understands you and is willing to enter your space for a while.

By the time Diana came home from work some three hours later Art and Sally were discussing next steps.

"Don't give in to him," Art was saying for the twentieth time as Diana rounded the corner. "He's a miserable little shit and is taking advantage of you. Don't you think Diana?"

"Don't I think what?"

And the story began again.

"It's not for me to say," mused Diana at the end of the long explanation. "But it does seem that Glen has more to lose than you if he shuts you out of his life. He would have to leave a comfortable home and find somewhere to live where he would have to pay his own bills. And he would lose access to a willing and able baby sitter."

"So you don't think I should give in?" asked Sally.

"No." Diana and Art spoke together.

Sally went to her course the next day. When she came home that evening she announced she was leaving in the morning.

"I've told Claude," she said. "I think he was a bit surprised but I said there were other more important things I needed to do than cut out bits of sugar paper."

"Good for you," said Art.

"No offence," she said. "You've been so kind. Even your house seems to want to help. You probably think I'm being ridiculous but there is something here that soothes the soul. Last night was so still that I started to hear my own voice again. For all that this has been the worst week of my life and I never want to see Minefield again."

They waved her off. "No repeat business there!" said Art. "If I got paid for the time I spent with Sally I'd be earning less than £1 an hour."

"I wonder what she meant about the 'house wanting to help'?" said Diana.

"You have to remember. She's nice but she is potty," said Art.

I know pride is one the deadly sins but I did feel just a little shimmer of the old self coursing around the walls.

* * * * * * * * *

About two weeks later there was a great hammering on the front door. A young man with a quiff and 'product'-greased hair, long pointy shoes and drain pipe jeans banged with his fist and shuffled around as if squaring up for a fight.

Diana came round the corner of the house.

"Hello."

"What have you been saying to my mum?"

"I'm sorry.."

"What have you been saying to my mum?" The tone was more agitated.

"Who is your mum?"

"Sally Brewster."

Diana took a breath and straightened her back. She put on her posh voice.

"You must be Glen," she said and reached out to shake his hand. "My name is Diana. I'm so pleased to meet you. Your mother spoke much of you when she was here but we haven't seen her since she left two weeks ago."

Glen, was nonplussed. Diana saw the young man visibly sag as the bluff and hot air went out of him. She had gained the upper hand.

"She's thrown me out," he said. "She's moved Paul in. It all happened after she came to stay with you. She's gone mad, the old trout. She keeps talking about a road to Damascus and seeing the light. So who is this f**king Damascus? Where is he? It's not fair."

Diana had this absurd desire to giggle and worked hard to keep a straight face.

"Look Glen. Whatever has happened with your mum has nothing to do with us. We just run a bed and breakfast. I'm sorry you've had a falling out but I do know your mum loves you. Possibly too much for her own good. So whatever happens I'm sure you will make up.

"Now, can I ask you to tone down both the language and the volume. It's not necessary here and it probably won't do you any favours with your mum."

"F**k off you old cow."

Glen turned to go and stomped back towards his car. I noticed it had been modified with wide wheels and a twin exhaust. There was a sticker on the back claiming sexual prowess. He flicked up the collar of his jacket in a gesture of defiance and opened the driver's door. The next thing we heard was a roar of anger as one of next door's white doves flew overhead and neatly deposited an in-flight package on his head.

Diana tried unsuccessfully to suppress a laugh. Glen turned round and took a step back towards her.

"Arternoon." A disembodied voice floated across the drive and Joe trudged into view en route to the allotments. "Everything OK?"

Glen looked at Diana and then at Joe. He launched a volley of expletives, got back in the car and drove off.

* * * * * * * * * *

About three months later another beautiful Sagrada Familia card arrived. This time it was post marked from Barcelona. It didn't say a great deal but it was signed from Mr Paul and Mrs Sally Stanley.

"I'd say that was a good investment of time on your part," said Diana.

"Still only £1 an hour," grumped Art. But I saw the secret smile even if Diana didn't.

Chapter Three: A Reunion

Minefield has a long history. There was probably a settlement here in the Iron Age. Certainly it was mentioned in the Domesday Book of 1086. The village has survived, thrived and shrunk across the centuries. At its height there were some 3,000 inhabitants. The reason? The Americans. The 353rd Fighter Group to be precise, followed by the 491st Bombardment Group. Around 2,700 of them joined the 300 Minefielders. Each night the High Street rang with the noise of American Jeeps, the sound of horns, the singing from the 4 public houses. Friday nights became regular dance nights. For 18 months the world of the quiet village was turned inside out. "Over sexed, over paid and over here" as the locals used to say.

The Americans certainly made their mark. Quite literally in fact. On a summer evening in July 1944 a bomb dump exploded. 1,200 tons of high-explosive and incendiary bombs rocked the countryside for miles around killing five men and destroying planes and equipment in the process.

Mrs Morgan, one of four pub landladies in the village, reported that her cousin had heard the explosion twenty miles away in Norwich. In Minefield virtually every window was blown out.

It was also in 1944 that an enemy aircraft dropped two bombs in Minefield. An unexploded one at the bottom of our meadow and another that blew up the house next door.

What then has all this to do with me or you dear Reader? Well a great deal really. Firstly because there were a number of connections made as you might imagine during that time and a few unexpected gifts were left at the end of the war.

Some weddings, some newborns and some cuckoos in the nest if rumour were to be believed.

The war babies growing up in the village, and those who came back to visit it, all had contact with the clergy and, by association, with me. The Vicarage became the first port of call for those researching family history or wanting to understand more about where their fathers, uncles and grandfathers had fought and lived. Throughout the 1970s, 80s and 90s there was something of a pilgrimage to the old airbases in East Anglia and stories of comradeship and courage were told in the very room in which bed and breakfast guests now stayed. But over the years the war veterans and their sons and daughters died and visits became less frequent.

Some of the Minefield girls went back to America as GI brides. Betty Squires, a barmaid from The Poacher public house was one such. For some the transition was hard. Many US families did not appreciate the new English brides. Others discovered that the clean cut war hero with the attractive accent and brash confidence was actually a very ordinary car mechanic or farm worker when back at home. Some girls, seduced by the promise of riches and big cars, found love faded away with the dreams. Some discovered only after they had reached the other side of the pond that there were already childhood sweethearts and even wives. Some travelled all the way to America but were never met and had to take the long sea voyage home alone. For all the heartbreak there were also some good marriages. Betty was one of those girls that made it work. In Minefield she was regarded as a good time girl but her natural optimism, sassy ways and sense of fun saw her through the hard times in the United States. She had ten children. All of them, at some point, made their way back to Minefield. They came to see where their father, Geoff, served as ground crewman for a Liberator known as Houston Sally and where their parents had met in 1944.

Betty never came back but she did keep in touch by letter with Mildred (or Millie as she was known) who had been a land army girl during the war. Betty died a much loved grandmother in 2004 and the family paid for our church bells to be rung every Thursday for a year in her memory.

There were a few children born out of wedlock who attended the local primary school where Mildred stayed as teacher and latterly head teacher. Mildred and the vicars worked closely together, it being a Church of England school. Minefield Primary, like many others, was built in Victorian times. It had the same white austere walls and heavy wooden single desks whose worn and carved lids bore the names of every pupil. Indoor toilets arrived in the late 1960s. In one of the many conversations I had with Minefield Primary he recalled the excitement of their arrival and the harsh, grease-proof toilet paper with every sheet monogrammed 'government property'. As with so many village schools numbers dwindled and Minefield Primary finally shut in the early 1990s when Mildred retired and the school register numbered six. It was a long way from the golden days when forty five children (eighteen during harvest time) would charge through the gates on a daily basis.

After the school shut the building was bought by a local potter. Business was not brisk and it now sits silent. Those curious enough to peek through the dusty windows, spy old cases of plates, bowls and china cups. Benign but lifeless. For a time I shared the same fate but thanks to Art and Diana I was beginning to feel new cement coursing through my veins. I wish the same luck to my old friend but for now he grows ever older as the spiders weave their cobwebs in silken sheets and the rooms slumber on.

Enough of these idle musings!!

As well as US airmen, we had Italian and German prisoners working on our farms. When the war ended a number of Italians stayed on. Their olive skin, sing song voices and silver tongues made them attractive and exciting in the eyes of Minefield women and there were quite a few marriages.

Lucas Pestalozzi was the result of one such liaison. His father, Eduardo, was a serial womaniser and the marriage was a tempestuous affair. After eight years Eduardo returned to Italy never to be heard of again. Mrs Pestalozzi was left to bring up Lucas alone. A proud woman she developed a prickly and defensive shell to ward off the perceived slights that came from firstly marrying an 'Itai' and secondly being abandoned by him. Lucas often came to school, unwashed and unkempt, and the children generally avoided him. As an adult he was something of a loner; preferring his own company to that of others, including his wife. At fifteen he went to work for Farmer Blowers, who was also a recluse, and it was there that he developed his fondness for pigs.

By the time the Old Vicarage Bed and Breakfast was established the transatlantic visits from veterans and their families had virtually dried up. Diana had done her best to make a few connections with some of the many groups and websites but had hit mostly brick walls. So it was a surprise to get an e-mail booking from a Frank Stockley. Frank was in his forties and was re-tracing family history. His grandfather had been in the 491st when it was at Minefield and Frank wanted to spend a couple of days in the village where his grandfather, Frank Snr, had been stationed.

"As far as buildings go, there's not much left to see," warned Diana as she showed Frank the room.

"Not a problem," said Frank. "I just want to soak up some atmosphere and perhaps talk to people who were around at that time."

"I'm afraid there won't be many alive now," said Diana.

"I was looking for someone in particular," said Frank. "Does the name Millie Tucker mean anything to you?"

"Millie Tucker ... Millie – oh do you mean Mildred Tucker? Surely not?"

"Mildred Tucker .... Could be ...... how old is she?"

"Well I don't know for sure but she must be in her nineties."

"Then that must be her. And does she still live here?"

"Yes, she's lives along the main street. She used to be headmistress of the primary school. Before my time I'm afraid so I'm a bit hazy on detail."

"What's she like?" asked Frank.

"Well I don't know her really. I think she's actively involved in the church group. She's regarded as pretty sharp. Um .. oh yes there was some controversy about her and the annual garden allotment quiz. Why do you ask?"

"My grandfather often talked about a Millie Tucker, especially in the final years after my grandmother had passed on. He used to get that faraway look that made me think there was something between them. When we asked he just said that Millie was a girl he met in England. He didn't give any more. Every time there was some news from England - say some political change - he would shake his head and say: 'Well Millie would approve of that or .. Millie wouldn't have wanted that.'"

"So you think ...... is it possible?" Diana's excitement was palpable.

"Dunno but I sure think it's worth finding out. Can you fix me an introduction?"

"Well I don't know Mildred very well but we can try."

The next day was Sunday. Frank and Diana walked up the village high street in the afternoon and knocked on Mildred's door.

Frank had spent the morning visiting the old runways that still cut through the fields surrounding the village. Not much remained from the war. An iron water tower, now a listed building, dominated the landscape and the village garage operated from an aircraft hangar. The rest of the buildings that housed those 2700 personnel had long gone except for an old brick latrine now encrusted with ivy. A war memorial, dedicated to the men of the 353rd and 491st, had been put up beside the main road on the outskirts of the village. These physical remains of a bygone period, together with the maps and historical records Frank had brought with him, helped to recreate the place where Frank Senior had lived, laughed and, perhaps, loved.

Mildred's house was a beautifully maintained cottage. Suffolk pink walls with climbing roses in full bloom and a garden full of summer flowers. Lupins, foxgloves and crocosmia mixed with cornflowers and poppies ensured a cascade of colour with just a hint of idiosyncrasy and wild abandon.

Diana knocked. They waited a couple of minutes and were just about to go when the sound of the door latch made them pause.

Mildred opened the door. Diana hadn't really seen her close up before. She was very thin, slightly bent and walked with a stick. Her white hair, lined face and apparent frailty defined her from a distance. But close up it was her piercing blue eyes that held you. She glanced quizzically at Diana and Frank and gradually her eyes fixed on Frank.

Later on Diana retold the story to Art.

"There was this long pause and I saw a look of recognition, confusion and then something like amazement and fear at the same time. She stretched out her hand towards Frank's face and then she just sagged and fell back against the wall. I thought she'd had a heart attack. Thank goodness Frank had more presence of mind than me. He rushed through the door and steadied her and then helped her into the living room and sat her in a chair. We got her a glass of water."

"What happened then?" asked Art.

* * * * * * * * *

"You look so like him," murmured Mildred.

"My grandfather. Frank Stockley. You did know him?" said Frank.

Mildred was rallying. "And who are you young man?" she asked.

"Ma'am. I'm sorry for your distress. My name is Frank Stockley jnr. I live in New Jersey. My grandfather – I have his picture here– was from Brooklyn, in the state of New York. He served with the 491st as a corporal and was stationed here in Minefield in 1944. People do say I look a bit like him. I'm staying with Diana and Art to find out more about his experiences in England. He often mentioned your name and I couldn't believe it when I heard that you still lived here."

"He still remembers me?" Mildred's voice shook slightly.

"Yes Ma'am, or rather he did. He passed away two years ago."

There was a heavy silence. Faraway memories now seemed like moments from yesterday. There were tears in Mildred's eyes when she spoke.

"Yes I knew your grandfather. He was a corporal. I was a land girl."

"Would it grieve you to tell me about him ..... you, ... that time?"

"It's all so long ago ... I don't know that I will remember much."

"Anything you can remember. I loved him very much. I've been planning this trip for a long time. To find someone who knew him then is just beyond belief. Please try..." There were tears in Frank's eyes this time.

There was a moment's silence. Mildred looked Frank over as if deciding whether she could bear to share some precious but painful memories.

After a little while, she spoke.

"Where's my stick?"

Diana handed it over and Mildred pulled herself up. "No don't fuss. I can manage. I've probably got a few pictures somewhere." She went over to her Globe Wernicke bookcases and opened the glass front. She pulled out an old photo album and brought it back to her chair.

"Where are my manners?" she muttered to herself. "Would you like a cup of tea?" she asked.

"Shall I get it while you talk?" asked Diana.

"Thank you Diana."

Mildred sat down again and looked at Frank. "Hmm ... got the same snub nose I see. Tell me do you have the same gift of the gab and the same brash confidence?" She was back in the driving seat.

"Grandfather was a New Yorker, Ma'am," said Frank. "And he was a salesman before he signed up. He could sell a fridge to an Eskimo."

Mildred laughed. "That was one of the refreshing things about your grandfather. He was slick, sharp, funny and so confident but he played jokes against himself as well. New York was the centre of everything. It was Jerusalem!! He had such self belief. Such a contrast from anyone I had ever met before. Of course all the Americans appeared that way but your grandfather particularly stood out. He ingratiated himself with everyone: men and women alike. He was always giving the village children sweets and chocolates. Wherever something was going on, he was in the thick of it."

"Sounds like grandad. So, Millie, how did you two meet?"

Mildred raised her eyebrows.

"You don't mind if I call you Millie?"

Mildred hesitated but the odds were against her. The face and cheerful grin before her brought back memories. They broke through a crust which had only ever been a thin veneer. She was the twenty four year old land army girl again with a craving for adventure and some fun.

"I was sent, along with five other land army girls, to work on the Peters estate around Minefield," she began, her blue eyes twinkling as she dusted off the memories. "I was from Plymouth and had never been so far north before. I'd also never worked on a farm. In those days it was a combination of horses and tractors. It's mostly arable around here but at that time there was a lot of cattle and I had charge of a herd of dairy Friesians. I used to collect them from the fields and bring them in for milking. That meant walking with them along Common Lane. Any traffic had to wait until I'd got them into the field. And that's how I met your grandfather. As you can imagine I wasn't at my ballroom best. I can still see him in the Jeep making wisecracks. I'm not sure he'd ever seen a cow before but when he made some comment about lady drivers I decided to take as much time as possible getting the cows down the road."

Frank laughed and passed Mildred a picture of his grandfather. One of those black and white photos showing a dark haired young man in a starched shirt with perfect teeth and an enormous grin. When Diana saw it she understood why Mildred had been so shocked. Frank jnr and Corporal Frank Stockley could have been brothers.

"The next time I saw him I was in the Poacher with the other land girls. He came over with some of his friends and asked if he could buy us a drink. I didn't think he recognised me but he made a beeline for me and well... Your grandfather could charm the birds from the trees. The rest is history. We had a glorious summer. It seems funny to say it given the war, but for me it was the best year of my life. It was so exciting. I felt as if I'd come alive, that I had something to offer to the war effort and I was in love. Of course we were very different and had so many arguments. I was essentially a socialist and he was an entrepreneur. I had that healthy British respect for class and he didn't believe in class. For him everything was possible."

Mildred looked up and saw the unasked question in Frank's face.

"You want to know what happened? Well Frank asked me to marry him. He wanted me to come back to America with him. But I wouldn't or couldn't go. I'd set my heart on being a teacher. I wanted to be part of building post war Britain. I had family here. Betty Squires, the barmaid from the Poacher, she took the risk and made it work. We corresponded regularly but it was very hard for her, especially in the beginning. Even though she was married she wasn't allowed the freedom that I had here in England as a spinster.

"If I had my time again … Frank, children… if I knew then what I know now …. Would I have gone? No I made the right choice. We both did. I never married. There was never anyone again who could live up to the light he brought into my life. That short time when I had it all.

"From time to time people remind me of Frank. Have you met Geordie Dave? He came with his family from Newcastle to live in the village. He's always looking for the next big idea just like Frank did. Falling flat on his face and getting up again."

Mildred fell silent lost in her memories. They waited until she looked up.

"So where's this tea?" she asked and smiled.

Frank, Mildred and Diana spent a couple of hours looking through the photos: at fresh faced and beautiful girls, the village as it has been in the war and pictures of American airmen including Frank.   There were a lot of laughs as Frank jnr related some of the scrapes his grandfather had got into back in New York, all the ideas and businesses he had tried and failed to get off the ground, the dance he had led their grandmother and the eternal optimism and humour they had all loved so much and for which so much had been forgiven.

By late afternoon, Mildred was clearly getting very tired so Diana and Frank took their leave. They walked in silence.

 "Thank you Diana," said Frank as they turned into my drive.

"My absolute pleasure," said Diana and the two hugged each other.

"Arternoon." Joe passed by the gate.

"Oh dear.. !!" said Diana. "Now it will be all round the village that I have a lover."

"Who leaves you here and goes back to America," laughed Frank. "Now. Where have I heard that story before?"

Chapter Four: The Mistress

"Tell you what," said Joe, the gardener, to Captain Adam as they stood looking at the chickens on the allotment. "The one staying at the moment is a corker. Nice little MG sports car too."

"When did you see her?" asked Adam.

"She arrived yesterday. I was coming down to feed the chickens and I saw her get out of the car. She's about 35, long dark hair, lots of make up, good legs. I wonder what she wants here? We haven't got any weddings or parties going on have we?"

"Don't ask me. I never know what's up. I rely on you to keep me informed."

The chicken co-operative was an important part of Minefield garden allotment life. About fifteen former battery hens were now roaming free within a huge meshed enclosure. Only seven people could be in the co-operative at any one time and each of the seven was assigned a day for eggs. There was a waiting list to join so it was a mystery to some how Adam had managed to get to the front of the queue. There were rumours of insider dealing and the exchange of some whacky baccy between Adam and Joe. Another unlikely couple who had found a shared interest.

Ms Porter was indeed attractive and glamorous.

"Put your tongue back in your mouth, Art," said Diana feeling that she didn't compare well.

"She's the sort of woman who knocks the idea of sisterhood and solidarity into a cocked hat. You keep hoping she's got varicose veins or some other imperfection," Diana later confided to her friend, Sue. "She completely ignored me and made a beeline for Art. It's as if she can't help herself. When she arrived she physically positioned herself between us with her back to me as if I didn't exist."

"How long is she staying?"

"Four days at the moment but could be longer. So I shall just keep biting my tongue and smile sweetly."

"Why is she here?" asked Sue.

"I don't know. She said it was for the walks and views. But so far she hasn't ventured outside her room and I don't think she's going to walk far with those heels. She just doesn't look the backpacking sort and she wasn't remotely interested in the woodpeckers and owls in the garden. I just don't see her as a natural country girl. I'm sure there must be something else going on."

Diana may have had some sixth sense or it may have been wishful thinking. Either way she was right. My walls have ears so I was getting the inside track on what was happening. It's just as well I have strong mortar or I might have blown my chimney stack.

Celine was on the phone as soon as the bedroom door was closed.

"Dickie – I'm here .... In Minefield ... At that ghastly B&B. ... You know the one misnamed The Old Vicarage. Run by Art something or other and his wife, a frumpy woman – can't remember her name."

I thought I could hear something between a snort and a roar at the other end of the phone.

"Now don't get cross sweetie pie… It's been a week since we last spoke, I thought this would be a nice surprise.

"No one need know. We could meet somewhere and have dinner. I'd certainly make it worth your while …

"Come on where is your sense of adventure?"

I could only hear strangled noises and hissing coming down the phone line. But after a few minutes and a mix of threat, seduction and some of that ridiculous adult baby-talk that humans tend to engage in when they are trying to get round each other, Celine and 'Dickie' finally agreed to meet.

It was the final sign off that got my windows rattling. "Over and out Wing Co," she giggled and switched the phone off.

"Dickie," "Wing Co". It could only mean one thing. That wretched Richard Wilfer was up to his old tricks again. Richard was the useless husband of my darling Jane, the heartbeat of the village. The woman who ran the shop, set up the choir, kept the village hall going and was generally at everyone's beck and call. When anyone new came into the village she would go a-calling with homemade cakes and biscuits, just to welcome them. Diana and Art were no exception. She was a familiar sight on her old bike come wind, rain or sunshine. She had lived in the village all her life and must be beckoning sixty now. She and Richard had married fairly late in life. She was forty and he was a bit older and heading towards retirement from the RAF with a good pension. They met through a friend of the family and it was more or less an arranged marriage with approval on all sides. Unlike many RAF wives she hadn't followed him around, preferring to stay in Minefield "where I can be useful."

As it happened the arrangement suited Richard perfectly. By all accounts he maintained his bachelor lifestyle while away, returning periodically to his comfortable home (Jane had inherited her parents' house) and a ready made social circle. He was a bit old school, not particularly bright or politically correct, all bluff and bluster with no interesting anecdote or conversation. Queen and country was his mantra. He was very susceptible to flattery and compliments and had a high opinion of himself as a lady's man which he continually undermined by blowing out his chest and guffawing inordinately at any female teasing.

Jane was well aware of her husband's imperfections and social gaffs but just accepted them. Through her good works, she had often visited us at the Vicarage and spent much time with the various vicars and their families. She was particularly friendly with one of my early vicars, Paul, his wife Sally and their three children. It was Jane who helped the family deal with the loss of their youngest child in a tragic road accident in the late 1970s: a drunk driver speeding too fast in the country lanes.

I remember on one occasion Richard had drunk too much sherry. He got louder and more raucous to the point where he was actually patted the bottom of Mrs Shreeve, the bishop's wife. Jane managed to get him home. She came round later to apologise: "He's such a klutz!"

"How do you put up with him?" asked Sally on another occasion when Richard had put his foot in it again.

"Oh Richard's heart is in the right place. And besides he would get himself into all sorts of pickles if I wasn't there to straighten things out."

And that, in a nutshell, was the answer. She'd spent her entire life being a saint: to her parents, to the vulnerable and needy in the village, to anyone who was in trouble. She just needed to be needed. Richard was a project and she was happy to take on someone that any other right minded woman would run a hundred miles from.

I had a soft spot for Jane and found her patience hard to accept. But Ms Porter was one step too far. Whatever romantic adventures Richard had or hadn't pursued in the past, he kept them away from the village. He wasn't a complete idiot. He did realise that his social standing and acceptability in Minefield was as part of a couple. So what was he playing at? And how had he managed to 'bag' such a beautiful creature. What on earth did she see in him?

I didn't have to wait long to find out.

The next phone call Ms Porter made was much shorter and more business like.

"Hi. It's me. Yes I've made the call. We're meeting tonight at the Magpie in Hassham. 7 pm. See you there. Bring the photos. There's mileage in this one. We can do the long squeeze."

The Magpie Inn in Hassham was a 16th century coaching inn. It was built of brick with timber beams and a charming Elizabethan courtyard. It had lots of nooks and crannies for private conversations. We got a lot of our intelligence on the comings and goings of local residents from the Magpie Inn jungle drums. Normally I wouldn't dream of listening to gossip and scandal. I have my standards. But this was Operation Jane so I sent an SOS and put the Magpie on alert.

7 pm on the dot Richard Wilfer walked into the bar room at the Magpie Inn.

"Hello Dickie my darling," cooed Celine. "I've ordered a whisky mac and set us up a tab."

"What are you doing here?" Richard barked in a fierce whisper. "You've booked into the village bed and breakfast. What if someone should see you? What if someone should see us? I have a position to maintain. What about my wife?"

"You mean you haven't told her about us? Oh Dickie you promised." The tears started to fall.

Dickie looked rather sheepish. "There, there my dear. Hear have a hankie. Things a bit tricky you know. Jane's a good old egg really. Need to find the right time."

"Don't you love me anymore? I thought we were so good together. We had such fun in Leicester at the convention. Oh Dickie!" Celine flung her arms around his neck. "I've missed you so much."

Dickie was getting distinctly uncomfortable. "Keep your voice down. Heat of the moment you know in Leicester. Often say things we don't mean .. what oh? Really didn't mean to lead you on. What say I pay your bill, bit of spending money, go back to Leicester?"

Celine opened her mouth to cry.

"E'vning." A disembodied voice floated out from behind the bar.

"Blast it. Now Joe's seen us," grumbled Richard getting hotter under the collar. "No chance of keeping it a secret now."

"Good evening Joe," he said. "Just out for a drink with my niece, Celeste. "Celeste meet Joe. He is a neighbour of ours in Minefield."

"Nice to meet you Celeste," said Joe, who no more believed this was Richard's niece than he could fly. "Lovely place for a drink. Do you mind if I join you?"

"YES!" they both said in unison, rather too loudly and too quickly. "Sorry old boy," added Richard. "We've got some private family matters to discuss."

"Not a problem," said Joe. "I was on my way out anyway. I've got some business to discuss myself." He meandered into the next bar.

"Celeste?" asked Celine.

"Oh damn it. It was the first thing I thought of. Look Celeste ... I mean Celine. I'm sorry I shouldn't have said those things. It's just not going to work."

"But we had such a good time, Dickie. Don't say it's over. I'm sorry I booked in at that tatty bed and breakfast. But when I hadn't heard from you for a week... Especially after all those texts ... I just couldn't wait. And now I come all this way and you just want to dump me because I'm an embarrassment."

She paused and gave him a coquettish glance. "Surely you remember the black stockings and the feathers?"

"Well ...." The whisky mac and the memory of a week "in flagrante" at a Leicester RAF re-union was beginning to take effect. With Joe gone, Richard was beginning to feel more reassured.

"They have rooms here you know," said Celine sensing her prey was weakening. "Big double beds.... For old times sake?"

Richard coughed a little as she squeezed his leg and brought her face close to his so that their noses could rub.

"Excuse me, Sir." They were interrupted by a man holding what looked like a menu.

"No thank you," said Richard. "I don't have much of an appetite, at least not for food." He chuckled, pleased with this own joke.

"Oh I think you will both want to see what's on this menu," the stranger said and handed him the leather bound folder.

Richard opened it, gasped and then shut it again.

"I'll leave you to have a look and then I'll come back and take your order." The stranger disappeared into the next room.

Richard went red with fury and his bulbous double chin seemed to quadruple in size over his bow tie. "What is it darling?" asked Celine.

Richard looked round to make sure that no one was watching them and then opened the folder again.

The photos were of the hotel room in Leicester where Richard and Celine had stayed. They were all taken from one angle, date and time stamped. It was clearly Richard and Celine and there were certainly some black silk stockings and a feather duster involved. In one photo Richard was tied to the bed.   Celine was standing over him wearing a short French waitress outfit with ridiculously high heels.

"Some waitress," grumbled the Magpie. "Discrediting the profession. She'd never have served soup without spilling it."   I'm not entirely sure the Magpie understood what he was describing. Bit single minded is the Magpie.

"What are we going to do?" Celine whispered. "If your wife sees these it will be the end of your marriage. If they get onto the internet you'll be a laughing stock. You'll lose face with your RAF friends and all your neighbours."

"You think I don't know that?" hissed back Richard.

"It's me in there too you know. My reputation and privacy destroyed too," Celine folded her arms tightly as she began to rock backwards and forwards.

Richard immediately looked guilty. "Yes, of course. I'm sorry. This affects us both. That was very ungallant of me. Don't cry Celi. Worse things happen at sea. What?!"   He didn't look like he could say exactly what might have been "worse".

"This is clearly blackmail. I wonder how much the blighter wants?" said Richard

"Whatever it is you will pay it won't you?   On a secretary's wages I don't have much and I spent most of my savings coming up to see you."

The next few minutes were spent in morose silence. The folder closed on the table between them. An embarrassing reminder of an old fool's peccadilloes.

The stranger came back. He was about 40. Despite the greying hair and slight paunch that sat atop his dark trousers and puffed out the waistcoat, there was still a remnant of youth and bygone fitness.

"So," he said drawing up a chair. "Are you ready to order?"

"These photos are taken using a digital camera," said Richard. "How do we know there aren't more or that they won't appear elsewhere or that you won't come back and demand more?"

"You don't. But I am a man of honour."

Richard snorted.

"There's no mileage in me coming back. Infidelity isn't the big deal it used to be. People are prepared to pay so much to get rid of the inconvenience but there is a limit. My job is to negotiate with you where that limit is."

"And if we call the police?"

"Why would you do that? It's as good as telling your wife. Besides where is your proof this conversation ever took place? No. You are buying an embarrassment-avoiding service here. I am just a service provider."

"Just tell us how much" Celi interrupted.

"£20,000."

Richard looked stunned. "How much?" he said weakly.

"£20,000. I'm not doing this for fun. I have to make a living you know. There are a number of expenses in my line of work."

"You piece of filth. If you think I'm going to pay you one penny. This is preposterous. Have you no scruples, man?"

The stranger raised his eyebrows. "You're asking me if I have scruples? Why do you think we are here?"

He let this sink in and continued. "Look old boy. You had a week of fun with the delightful Miss Porter. For all I know, or care, you can carry on with the stockings and feather dusters. I believe there was a paddle in one of the later photos. But this time you got caught out. So just pay up and accept it as part of the game. Incidentally, it's not just still photographs. There is a video with sound."

Celine and Richard looked stunned.

"Oh Dickie. Just pay this hateful man and let's get him out of our lives," Celi urged.

Richard had visibly sunk at the mention of the 'video'. He knew he was beaten and he knew, although it would sting, that he could get his hands on £20,000 without Jane asking too many questions.

He was about to try and negotiate a lower price when a strong female voice from behind the trio said, "Excuse the interruption. I'd like to speak to Mr Davey."

They all turned round to see a uniformed police woman and another man in plain clothes. No one had even seen them walk in. It was a bit like a game of chess, the Magpie reflected as he relayed the events to me. You can get so intent on your own game plan you fail to notice the knight threatening your queen.

The blackmailer craned his neck as if seeking a possible escape route.

"My name is Davey. And this is a private conversation. Can it wait?"

"I'm afraid not," said the uniformed officer. "Although I would have been fascinated to hear what was coming next.

"Mr Davey I am arresting you under section 21 of the 1968 Theft Act for the offence of blackmail. You do not have to say anything but it may harm your defence if you do not mention when questioned something which you later rely on in court. Anything you say may be given in evidence."

The plain clothes man stepped forward and beamed at the group. "I'd come quietly and without any fuss, Mr Davey. Or would you prefer we called you Mr Stewart? Take him away please, Constable?"

Mr Davey got up quietly and started to walk towards the exit. Just as he got to the door he turned his head and glanced at Richard. "I didn't think you of all people would have the balls," he said.

There was a silence as he left the room. Celine got up. "I think I need to wash my face," she said.

"Not so fast Miss Browning," said the plain clothes officer.

"My name is Celine Porter."

"Good I'll add it to the list of aliases."

Another uniformed office appeared and Celine was also promptly arrested and marched off. As the Magpie later said all this activity was worth more than a year's advertising in the Hassham Express.

Richard was beginning to look as if he might have a heart attack. "What … what ..where. … who …"

"Are you alright Sir?" The plain clothes officer sat down. "You've had a bit of a nasty shock I would guess."

"Where did you come from? Who are you? Where have you taken Celine?"

"My name is Inspector Mostly," said the plain clothes officer. "I work for Leicestershire CID." He showed his ID. The police officers you saw are from Norfolk Constabulary. I realise that this has all been a bit sudden. First blackmail and then the immediate arrest of the perpetrators. I'm afraid you are not the first. If you'd like to come to the Diss police station and give a witness statement I'll explain all."

"The police station? Oh er .."

"You might find it a bit more private, Sir," said Inspector Mostly.

"Yes, of course," said Richard.

My contacts don't extend as far as Norfolk police stations who don't know the meaning of give and take. Luckily the local police officers often drink in the Magpie and so the story unfolded. Richard was just another in a long line of deluded older men who had been seduced by Linda Browning (Celine) and subsequently blackmailed.

It all came to an end when the Bonnie and Clyde of East Midlands misjudged one of their other victims. Mr Longface. Initially he had paid up like everyone else but his wife found out anyway and collected evidence through a private investigator. Her revenge took the form of ritual and public humiliation including shredded suits and significant credit card usage. She paid a local graffiti artist to paint a mural of her husband's exploits in the local underground station and arranged for flyers to be pasted on every car in his office car park. At this point, with nothing to lose, he complained of the blackmail to the local police.

It didn't take the police long to find Browning and Davey. At the time Linda was in the middle of her seduction of Richard. So they let it run to catch the blackmailers 'red handed'.

Richard was most anxious that Jane wouldn't find out and was torn between 'doing his duty' and denying that anything had happened. Eventually he was persuaded to do the honourable thing helped, no doubt, by the reduced risk (the case would be dealt with in Leicester) and the threat of home visits for follow up questions.

And so Richard had got away with it. Again. Except....

* * * * * * * * * *

"It was most peculiar," Diana said to Art as they worked together pulling brambles from the front hedge. Joe, who just happened to be passing, stopped to listen.

"I knocked on the door and Jane answered. We did the 'hello, how are you thing'. Then I said that Celine had left some rather nice earrings in the room. Joe told us she was Richard's niece and did they have a forwarding address? Jane looked completely blank. Then she seemed to freeze and finally she called Richard out from the lounge."

"Richard, darling," she said. "Diana has brought round Celine's earrings."

"Richard went bright red and just starred at us all. He didn't say anything and I thought he was going to collapse. Then Jane said: 'ah Celine'. Just like that. She said she would take the earrings and pass them on. It was most peculiar."

"So if she wasn't his niece, who was she?" said Art.

Joe grinned from ear to ear. "I'd love to have been a fly on the Wilfers' wall that evening," he said.

Chapter Five: The Great Escape

Most of the people who stay with us want the full works. They want a full English breakfast. They want to wander round the garden and Ash Meadow. They want to be enchanted by the bantam chickens, Faith, Hope and Charity, bouncing across the lawn and to see the squirrels racing up and down the trees.

Vince Harris wanted none of these. He was a stocky man in his late forties with snake tattoos hugging his arms and neck and a Newcastle accent. He was a sharp dresser, walked with a slight swagger and drove a rather expensive looking Subaru Impreza. Art wondered why he would choose to stop at their bed and breakfast rather than a smart hotel.

"Are you here for business or pleasure?" he asked as he showed Vince the room.

"Bit of both I should think."

"Perhaps you know Dave Aldridge?"

Vince wheeled round to face Art. "What makes you say that?"

"A calculated guess based on your accent. His family is the only one in the village who speak like you and people don't usually stay here unless they have some local connection."

Vince visibly relaxed and laughed. "I suppose the accent does stand out a bit to your ears, man. But last time I spoke to Dave he had lost his."

Art laughed too. "It's not as strong as yours but round here it sticks out like a sore thumb."

"He doesn't know I'm here. I'm going to surprise him. It's been a long time. There's a wife and one bairn?"

"I think there are three children now. An older boy and two younger girls."

"And his missus, Kate? Is she well?"

"Oh yes. The whole family are good. Into everything. Part of the heart and character of the village. You northerners have an energy we don't have here. An evening with those two and I'm reaching for the ibuprofen!!"

That seemed to break the ice. Vince asked a few questions about the village, how big it was and how many visitors it attracted.

"It's pretty isolated here," he commented.

"That's what BT says when giving reasons for our weak broadband signal. But we're not that far from civilisation. It's not like we are at the top of a mountain in the Highlands of Scotland. Sometimes on a day with a good wind and a willingness to stand on one leg you can even get a mobile phone signal."

Vince glanced at his phone. "It's weak but there is still a pulse," he said.

"No offence," he continued, "but I won't be wanting any breakfast and I don't want my room cleaned. I'll leave towels outside the room if I want them changed. I really do want total privacy. I need to spend some quality time on my own just now. I'll pay you in advance for five days and then leave the key when I go. Is that OK?"

"Of course, whatever you want. If you need thinking time then feel free to use the garden and meadow to get a change of scene. This is a nice big room. But five days in here and you'll go stir crazy."

"Cheers. Another time I'll be much more sociable. It would be nice to get to know you all."

* * * * * * * * *

"So what's he like?" asked Diana. Her curiosity piqued.

"Just a bloke. Nice enough. He wants to be left alone."

"I wonder why?"

"To get away from people asking questions like that, I expect!"

It might have been a different conversation if they had seen what I saw.

* * * * * * * * *

After Art left, Vince locked the door and then looked out of the window. The room was at the front of the house. There was a fairly big parking area that led down to a gate and then out on to the road. Vince continually glanced around as he picked up his case, laid it on the bed and opened it.

He took out two neatly pressed shirts, a couple of pairs of trousers and some underwear. Underneath, neatly packed in rows were what looked like 1lb bags of a white powder. Either Vince used a lot of sugar substitute or this was cocaine.

He looked at the packages, picked out a couple and turned them over before putting them back. He closed the case and put it on top of the wardrobe. Then he sat on the bed and just stared into the distance for a while. Eventually he pulled out his phone, took a piece of paper from his pocket and dialled a number.

"Hello. Is that Dave? You'll never guess? Vince. Vince Harris. No, I'm not joking. I'm in Minefield at your local B&B. Is that anywhere near you? Man, what's happened to your voice. Have you gone posh? No that's fine. You finish what you're doing and I'll see you later. It's been a long drive. I could do with a rest."

He snapped the phone shut, took his jacket off and lay down on the bed. Within minutes he was sound asleep.

Dave came round at 7 pm. They hugged. The kind of embrace that suggested a past and genuine affection between the two men. "You should have phoned," said Dave. "We'd have found somewhere to put you up."

"I don't remember Kate being overly keen on me," said Vince.

"It wasn't you, man. It was the life. We lived in the blurred part between right and wrong. Bit of scamming here. A few dodgy deals there. But the net was drawing in and when the boy came along, she wanted him to have something different with fewer temptations. In the end I had to make a choice."

"We had some laughs though. Don't you miss it?"

"I miss the buzz. The cars, the speed, the lads. But it was the right choice. The kids have grown up safe and Safie, my youngest, is as bright as a button. The teachers say she could easily go to university. That would be a first for us.

"So what's it to be?" said Dave. "A night on the bevy? Come and have something to eat with us and meet the family." The enthusiasm was genuine and it was infectious.

Vince grinned. "Lead on," he said.

* * * * * * * * *

Vince rolled in about 3 am the next morning and at midday he opened his eyes, groaned and clutched his head, clearly the worse for wear. He spent 20 minutes in the shower but it didn't shift the headache so he went outside and found Art cleaning out the chickens.

"You wouldn't have some aspirin, would you mate?" he asked.

"I'm sure I can find some," said Art. "You did a lot of quality thinking last night then?"

"Some of my best ideas have been found at the bottom of a whisky glass."

"You must have found a lot of inspiration last night!! Dave has been round twice but he couldn't knock you up. He says he'll come again later today."

"Cheers," said Vince as he downed the pills and water. "Couldn't trouble you for a coffee I suppose?"

And that's where Dave found them both, rolling with laughter in the back garden sharing jokes and anecdotes.

"This is a good place to be," said Vince. "I can see why you didn't leave when you found it. It's a long way from the real world, a sort of bubble." He sighed. "Jeez I'm too old for regrets."

"Art. It's been great crack to meet you," he continued. "But Dave and I have some business to discuss. Will you excuse us?"

"Of course. I'd better get on. Diana will be back soon. She might just notice nothing has been done and then I'll be for it!"

"Ah the lovely ladies, what would we do without them?"

Vince took Dave back to his room.

"I'm in a spot of bother," he said.

Dave looked at him. "I knew it," he said. "So whose husband is after you now? He must be important. You'd usually be out of range in Whitby."

"It's not the lasses this time," said Vince and he took down the case and opened it.

"Jesus," said Dave. "Tell me that's not what I think it is."

"Cocaine."

"How much is there?"

"Street value probably £1.5 million."

"And it's yours?"

"Well not technically."

There was a micro pause while Dave took this in and then he exploded.

"You've stolen £1.5 million of cocaine from God knows who and brought this shite to my door. What the f**k did you think you were doing? Who does it belong to? Give it back."

"It's not that easy. It sort of fell off Mr Hanrohan's lorry."

"Hanrohan? Shit!" Dave collapsed into a chair.

"It's why I didn't come and knock on your door. I didn't want to bring this into your house. Not with the kiddies and all."

"That's f**king big of you." Dave was getting wound up.

"Keep your voice down for Christ's sake."

"Do they know you've got it?"

"I expect they've worked it out by now."

"Hanrohan's got fingers in every pie. He'll be tracking you down as we speak. You're not exactly inconspicuous. Mobile phone, credit cards, flashy car. I'm surprised you didn't have a neon light with a big arrow made." Dave went to the window as if expecting to see mobsters with machine guns under every tree advancing to the house.

"Do you think I'm a complete idiot? PAYG phone, cash only and I found the car."

"You've stolen the car?!" Dave was incredulous.

"I needed to get away."

"You need banging up in a loony bin. OK. You're here now. You and a bent motor and £1.5 million of cocaine. What next?"

There was silence.

"You haven't got a clue, have you?" said Dave.

"I'm mulling over a few ideas," said Vince defensively. Then. "Oh come on Dave. You are my last chance. You always had the answers. You always had a plan."

"If Hanrohan comes down here. It won't just be you he takes out it will be all of us. You don't think he won't be combing through the files, checking out all your old contacts? £1.5 million. He won't take that lying down. Oh my God. You've got to go. This is nothing to do with me."

"Where am I going to go?" asked Vince. "You said it. Eyes everywhere. At least lying low here I can buy some time. I go somewhere else and I'm at risk. I know I've got to leave the country and I figured you might know how. I didn't mean for this to happen. It was a transfer that went wrong. Suddenly I had more money than I've ever seen and a chance to start again. Maybe I shouldn't have come here. I didn't mean to put your family in danger. But you know me – act now, think later. It's in all our interests that I disappear and I need you to help me do that."

"What do I know?" said Dave. "I don't have contacts for this kind of thing around here. That's what I moved to get away from. I can't help. You have got to leave. If you don't I'll phone Hanrohan myself and tell him where you are."

The words were out. A tense and chilly silence fell. "You'd do that?" Vince sounded broken.

"This isn't some big game. If it's my family or you, my family wins every time," blustered Dave.

"I thought I was family," said Vince.

"Don't go there."

"How many times back in the day did I pull your arse out of the fire? When Kevin got shot. Who was there for you?"

A long silence. The two men stared at each other. The messages and memories soundlessly transmitting backwards and forwards.

Eventually. "Perhaps you can get me a boat?" suggested Vince.

"A boat. Where the f**k do you think I'm going to get a boat from?"

A rumble from the road and the sound of some brakes brought them both to the window.

It was a tractor loaded with hay pausing in the drive to let a car pass.

"Jesus. This is like playing Russian roulette," said Vince. "Every time I hear something I think my number is up."

"How long do you think you've got?" asked Dave.

"I don't know. A day. Maybe longer. You know if Hanrohan catches up with me he won't just kill me. Hanrohan will want to send a message." The bravado was gone.

"You're right I had no right to bring you into this or risk your family," Vince continued. "I'll head towards London and take my chances there."

"Who do you know in London? And don't you think that the minute you open your mouth you will stand out like a bishop in a brothel?"

"I'll take my chances. But it's a bit difficult to disguise my voice."

There was another silence. And then Dave got up. This time Vince could tell it wasn't blind panic.

"You've got that look. I knew it. You've got that look!! You haven't lost it."

"Give me five hours. Don't move outside this room. I'll be back."

Vince spent the intervening time watching television, looking at his watch and drinking coffee.

* * * * * * * * * *

Dave returned inside the five hours.

"OK. I've pulled a few strings. Begged a few favours. Get ready to go."

"Whey – eh man. Ready to rumba. Where are we going?"

"We (as in you and I) are not going anywhere. You are going on a short ride and then a mate of mine will take you to his boat. You'll be crewing for him. You've got your passport?"

"Yes. What do you mean I'll be crewing for him?"

"He takes luxury boats around the world for their owners. He's taking this one to Malta."

"But I've only ever been on one of those pedalo things. I get seasick at the thought of a ferry."

"Do you need to get out or not?"

"Alright, alright. Keep your hair on. I was only saying."

Vince's face began to lighten. "Hey up. In two week's time I'll be sipping pina coladas on sun kissed beaches surrounded by beautiful women."

He leapt on the bed and pumped up some pillows. "What have you told this mate of yours?"

"Only that you're in trouble and need to get away for a while."

"How does he explain me as a crew member?"

"He has to register the crew but you can be listed as a late substitute. You're not in trouble with the police, only with Hanrohan."

"What about the gear?"

"He doesn't know anything about it and he doesn't need to."

"You're a great pal. If I'd realised it was this easy. I'd have done it years ago."

"Hanrohan has a long reach. You won't be able to come back."

Vince nodded as serious as it appeared he was ever likely to be. "I'm turning my back on this life, Dave. I've got this far without prison or long term injury. This is no life for a man approaching fifty."

He grinned. "I could open a beach bar. I've always fancied that, man. Find a local lady. Settle down."

"You? Settle down? Now that would be worth seeing."

"Thanks Dave," said Vince. The two men looked sheepish as if working out whether it was OK to touch. Vince put out his hand and the two men hugged.

Dave's mobile rang. It was Kate.

"Dave, someone just rang. They asked if we had seen Vince. When I said he was round last night, they asked where he was staying. I didn't like the tone, so I said I didn't know but … Something's up isn't Dave? It always is when Vince is around."

Dave pushed a hand through his hair and began pacing up and down. "Nothing that I know of Kate. Honest. Would I lie to you? Did he say where he was calling from? Oh – just to tell Vince to get in touch. Did he leave a name or number? Vince would know who he was. OK. I'll pass it on."

Dave hung up.

"Shit! Shit! Shit!"

He looked at Vince.

"Hanrohan's on his way."

"Oh Christ!"

"We've probably still got time," said Dave who sounded calmer than he must have been feeling. "They're probably driving down, opening the local ears and eyes. It will take a few hours to get here and Joe will be arriving with our transport in half an hour."

"What about the car?"

"Forget the f**king car. I'll deal with it. Where did it come from?"

"Kenny White."

"Not Kenny White as in right hand psycho of Hanrohan?"

"The keys were in the ignition."

"You pillock!"

The next twenty minutes were nail biting for all of us. Every time a car passed we expected it to reverse and screech into the drive.

Finally at 7.30 pm we heard the sound of a heavy vehicle pulling off the road at the front of the drive.

Dave looked out. "OK. Good to go." He motioned to Vince who came forward.

"It's a tractor!" he said.

"No flies on you."

"It's got a trailer load of hay bales."

"Your carriage awaits."

"I ask for a get away car and he brings me a f**king tractor."

"Stop bleating and get moving," said Dave.

Joe was out of the tractor and moving one of the bales.

Vince opened the front door and suddenly stopped. "The case," he said and laughed. "I nearly forgot."

"You and the case part company here," said Dave.

Vince stared at him as if he had misheard. "What .. ," he started.

Dave cut in. "You came for my help. That's fine. You brought our past into my present. That's not fine. It's what I came to get away from. So the deal is 'no drugs'. I'm helping you. I'm not getting involved with anything else."

"What are you going to do with them?"

"Get rid of them."

Vince hesitated, weighing everything in the balance. And then … one of his big grins.

"Oh f**k it. Easy come, easy go." He ran out of the house, down the drive and leapt head first into the hole Joe had made for him in the hay bales.

"Thanks mate," said Dave as Joe plugged the hay hole.

"What for?" Joe asked. "I'm just delivering some hay."

* * * * * * * * * *

The next day there was a loud banging at the door.

Art went to answer it, and found a large, pockmarked man outside. In the drive was a beautiful black BMW with two other men sitting in it.

The man spoke with a Geordie accent. "I'm looking for Vince Harris," he said with a smile. A golden crown glinted in the side of his mouth.

"I'm afraid he's gone," said Art feeling quite relieved and not knowing exactly why.

"Where to?"

"I'm not sure exactly," said Art. "He said he was staying for five days but he left last night. His mate Dave told me he had decided to leave. He said something about Southampton. Would that make sense?"

The man seemed about to ask another question when they were both stopped by a pecking sound coming from the car.

"Oh I'm so sorry," said Art. I'm afraid it's the mad crow. He's seen his reflection in the car and he's trying to fight himself."

"Hey, get off." Pockmark ran back to the car and the crow took off. "Pesky f**king bird," he said.

"What car was he driving?"

Peck, peck, peck.

"I'm afraid he won't stop," said Art. It might be an idea to get the car on to the road if you don't want him to do some damage to the body work."

Pockmark seemed torn between wanting to interrogate Art further and saving his car. In the end the car won.

"Thank you for your time," he said. "If Vince does get in touch can you call me on this number?" He handed over a card with his name and mobile. Kenny White.

"No problem," said Art.

He watched the BMW reverse out, looked at the card and slowly tore it up. "Hell can freeze over before I call you," he murmured to himself.

* * * * * * * * * *

A few days later Art was flicking through the TV channels and hit on the local news.

"Police report that a suitcase of cocaine, with an estimated street value of £1.5 million, was found by a local dog walker on Dunwich beach. They are appealing for witnesses. Locals say smuggling is rife in the area and that it may have come across from the Netherlands."

"Now why doesn't anything exciting like that happen in our area?" he said to no one in particular.

Chapter Six: Lily the Ladybird

"Oh yes, it's really taken off in New Zealand," Karl said as he stirred his tea and took another slice of the lemon polenta cake Diana had baked. "Our Lily the Ladybird stories are used as part of the school curriculum to support reading so that really helps. If we could just get them to take over here or the United States we would be made."

"But this wasn't just about the money," added his wife Charlotte, a tall willowy woman in her mid fifties. "It was a life style choice so we could work together."

"So what were you doing before?" asked Diana who was drinking in every word.

Karl puffed out this chest. "Oh I was a TV script writer. Casualty, bit of Coronation Street, couple of episodes of The Bill. I worked on some of the early Morse series."

"Did you get to go on set while they were filming?"

"Oh sometimes. To help with the re-writes. But now our focus is on children's books. So much more rewarding."

"Do you both write?"

"Karl is the writer," said Charlotte. "I'm just the researcher."

"That doesn't feel like a 'just' job," said Diana.

"Charlotte works for me, keeps me going, brings me cups of tea. She's my right hand." Karl beamed at his wife.

"Was it difficult to get established?" asked Diana. "To be able to earn enough to work at it full time?"

"Oh yes. Getting started was horrendous. But we decided it was an itch I had to scratch. So for a couple of years I just shut myself away and wrote and badgered people. We lived in penury, didn't we darling? The small pittance from your dreary job .."

"I worked as an archivist in the British Library," said Charlotte. "It was quite interesting really .."

"And then I finally got some work accepted and the whole thing snowballed from there."

"It must have been a big change and risk to give up the TV writing and focus on children's books. I imagine that's just as competitive." Diana was really intrigued.

"Well if something really juicy and tempting came up, I might be persuaded to take it," said Karl. "But it would have to be good to tear me away from the idyllic life we have now on Guernsey. Away from the London rat race."

"How did you get the idea for Lily the Ladybird?"

"It was something we came up with together, wasn't it?" said Charlotte.

"Yes," admitted Karl. "You were playing about with the character. Got a book published which did quite well for a first attempt and then I moved it forward to where it is now; internationally renown. A children's classic you might say."

"This is so exciting for me," said Diana. "I hope you don't mind me asking you these questions. I've always wanted to write a book. I know they say that everyone does. But to meet someone who's gone beyond the dream and actually made it." Diana realised she sounded quite star struck but couldn't stop herself.

"Not a problem. We don't mind talking about it," said Karl. "You'll have to look up our books on the internet. It's nice to reflect, sometimes, just how far we've come."

"So what brings you down here?" asked Art who had joined them on the patio. The sun was beginning to burn through the early morning mist and it was turning into a really lovely July weekend.

"Our agent. He lives in the next village. He's having a birthday bash and we've all come to celebrate," Charlotte responded.

"Oh that's lovely – to have a good personal as well as a professional relationship," Art said politely.

"In this business, you can't survive without a good agent," said Charlotte.

"Talking of which …. I suppose we better go and get changed if we are going out," said Karl.

After they left Diana turned to Art. "How exciting," she said. "A real life writer."

"Their relationship was a bit funny," said Art.

"I suppose she was a bit subservient," conceded Diana.

"Especially as it appears she kept him while he got established and she wrote the books that now keep them. Did you see how dismissive he was of her work in the British Library? And he smelt of alcohol."

"Are you sure? I didn't notice. I take it you didn't like them?"

"Oh she was fine. It's him I didn't like. Big headed. Has-been."

"What do you mean Has-been?"

"Well…. For a start all those shows he claims to have scripted are decades old. What's he done recently?"

"The children's books. You heard *'Lily the Ladybird'*."

"Oh yeah. You really think someone like him who enjoys the limelight so much would just give it up to write children's books? It doesn't ring true. There's more going on there. And if they are so well off, why come to stay with us? Why not stay with their agent?"

"Well it depends on how many people are coming and we are quite close." But Diana could see that Art had a point.

Art got up. "Well I guess we'll never know. Still it doesn't matter to us, does it? Money in the till."

Art was right about one thing. Karl took out his hipflask as soon as they got back to the bedroom.

"What ghastly people," he said. "Small minds, parochial thinking. What are we doing here?"

"I thought Diana was quite sweet," said Charlotte. "And that lemon cake was to die for."

"But what are we doing here? We should be staying with George. Fifteen years ago we'd have been at the centre of the party, not stuck in some pokey, backwater bed and breakfast. What does he mean, he hasn't got room? There's bags of room in his place."

"But he has lots of people coming and we weren't on the first round of invites."

"And that's another thing. Why not? If I hadn't let you talk me into giving up the TV scripts and moving to the back of beyond in Guernsey, we would never have been forgotten."

Charlotte was going to say something but then didn't bother. She had apparently learned that sometimes it was better just to say nothing.

By the time Karl had showered and changed, his mood was much improved.

"Sorry darling," he said. "Just a bit nervy. … Come on let's go and wow them with our wit and repartee. I'm feeling on form."

They kissed and by the time they left the room, they were the best of friends again.

* * * * * * * * *

We next saw them about 1.30 am. Karl was in high spirits and on good form. "Roll out the barrel," he warbled. He lay on the bed while Charlotte pulled off his socks and shoes.

"We're back in, Charlie girl. No more crappy Lily the Ladybird books. Back to the adult stuff. God it's good to be back with the crowd. So much happening. I've missed so much living in the middle of nowhere and I'm back with the groove. I'm going to have a piece of the action. That new police drama sounds particularly juicy. We need to move back to London. No question. We were mad to leave. No wonder we're out of the loop. Waiting for the phone to ring. We have to get in there and pitch alongside everyone else.   Lily the Ladybird!! Huh!! What a waste of my bloody talent."

"I thought you were proud of what we'd achieved." Charlotte seemed a little subdued. "You certainly sounded like you were today."

"Making a silk purse from a sow's ear. That's the writer's craft. Turning water into wine. Anyone can write children's books. You proved that. The real stuff is in the drama. That's where reputations are to be won and made. And now we have a chance to get back in there."

"It's only a meeting with George. We don't know where it's going."

"Yes but when is the meeting?   At the end of the day. When we can get a bit of peace and quiet. After everyone's left. He knows how much I want a piece of the action. I've told him enough recently."

"I didn't realise you'd had regular contact."

"Just a few texts and phone calls. He's been tricky to track down. This party was a gift from the gods. Pin him down. That was my strategy. And it's worked.   We'll put the house on the market when we get back."

"I thought you were happy with our lives in Guernsey?"

"Charlie. I've been sleep walking and I'm just waking up. I've been treading water. I'm feeling energised and ready to go. I haven't felt so alive in years. You wouldn't want to deny me that would you? We'll soar into the heavens together."

"As long as you don't go too close to the sun," murmured Charlotte.

"You want to bring that up again?" The mood had changed. "For Christ's sake. That's in the past. Over. Done with. A one off. Your problem is you're just boring, no taste for adventure. You with your filing, your meticulous research, your Lily bloody Ladybird."

Charlotte was finally stung. "I don't want to row, Karl, but Lily the Ladybird has given us a stable living."

"One horse jockey. Boring. Boring. Boring. What do we know about kids? We don't even have any."

There was silence.

"Jesus Charlie. I'm sorry. It's just the drink."

Charlotte sat heavily on the bed, head bowed.

Karl was all solicitous. He put his arms around her. "Sweetheart. Don't listen to me. It's just the drink and all the excitement of a new life beckoning. Forgive me. Come to bed." He kissed her cheek and lay back down. Five minutes later he was asleep.

I noticed it took a lot longer for Charlotte to fall asleep. She lay beside him, eyes open, staring at the ceiling. I watched the tears trickle from the corners of her eyes. After a while she curled up into a foetal position and rocked herself to sleep.

I felt for her as I watched her turning in her sleep. How must it feel to know that for decades you have tied yourself to someone unworthy of your love? Charlotte had been alongside Karl, every step of the way, sacrificing her own career and interests to his. And in the darkness of the night she was once again balancing the love and pain, realising that she might have another thirty years with this stranger she called husband. I saw the tension in her face as she thought of all the pathways there might have been, all the missed opportunities and wondered if the die was now irrevocably cast.

The next day at breakfast Karl was, in his words, 'cooking on gas'. Everything was wonderful. The bed was the best he had ever slept in. He took delight in the bantam chickens scampering across the lawn and in the squirrels that swung Tarzan-like from tree to tree. He even remembered that Diana had said she was interested in writing and asked her a few questions.

"Although I'm not sure he actually listened to anything I said," she later confided in Art. "Charlotte was a bit quiet though."

"From my lowly position in the kitchen, I don't see how she could have got a word in edgeways," said Art.

"He said it was a big day for him. He was meeting with his agent to talk about his next writing project. No wonder he's bubbling with excitement."

* * * * * * * * *

It was about 5 pm when they heard the gravel scrunching as the little mini convertible pulled onto the drive.

Diana and Art were pulling up nettles from under the Leylandii hedge.

Diana crawled out backwards. "I wonder if we'll find out tomorrow what the project is?"

They heard the slamming of the car door and then the front door banged shut. The next thing they heard was raised voices.

"I'm no Sherlock Holmes," said Art. "But I don't think the meeting with their agent went very well."

"Do you think I should offer them a cup of tea?" asked Diana.

"No!!" said Art.

Inside the house, Karl was ranting.

"Bastard!" he shouted. "That f**king bastard wouldn't recognise talent if she got up and swiped him with her handbag. He doesn't feel he is the best person to be my agent. Lazy little shite!! I helped make him."

"He is right though. His focus isn't really children's books," began Charlotte.

"You still just don't get it, do you? I am trapped by Lily the bloody Ladybird. I want something different. He offered me nothing!"

"We'll find someone else."

"This is just what you wanted isn't it? To trap me in that mind numbingly dull world of yours. Have you engineered this? Have you been speaking to George behind my back? You think I'll come back to Guernsey and be your 'yes –man'.

I used to be someone. Thanks to you I've lost my contacts and now even my agent. You've dragged me down to your level of mediocrity and you expect me to thank you for it. You witch. Well the scales have fallen. I see your game."

He stormed out of the house, slamming doors on the way. The car tyres crunched again on the gravel as it left the drive.

Charlotte went white with shock. She rolled over onto the bed and held her stomach, rocking backwards and forwards as if in physical pain, tears rolling down her cheeks.

I thought I should intervene. I hate to see humans in this much pain. So rightly or wrongly I closed off all sound from the road, allowing only the birdsong to seep through the walls. It was a trick I often used when I was a proper vicarage. I cocooned this unhappy lady in silence.

An hour passed and gradually Charlotte uncurled and sat up. She made herself a coffee and went outside into the glorious July sunshine. She spent another hour just wandering around the meadow and in amongst the trees of the little orchard at the back of the house.

When she came back she went into the bathroom and applied some foundation to cover the tearstains on her face. She phoned for a taxi and then went to find Diana.

"Something has come up and I have to leave," she said.

"Oh I'm sorry. Is there anything I can do?" Diana thought it better to see all, hear all and say nothing. She was learning.

"No but I just wanted to pay you for the stay. In case Karl forgets to do so when he comes back."

Art and Diana waved her off and looked at each other. "Another happy customer!!" he said.

About 11 pm they were watching television when they heard the mini come back into the drive and Karl's voice calling for Charlotte. He was clearly the worse for wear.

Art went out to see him.

"Charlotte had to go mate," he said. "Something's come up. She took a taxi."

"I'd better go after her," slurred Karl.

"I think you'd better go to bed tonight and catch up with her in the morning." Art was firm but diplomatic.

Karl allowed himself to be propelled in the direction of the bedroom.

"He was running on about betrayal and ladybirds," Art reported.

"Will there be any trouble?" asked Diana anxiously.

"No," said Art. "All mouth, that one." He looked affectionately at Diana. "Sorry to puncture your illusions. He's as messed up as the rest of us."

Karl left the next morning without breakfast and without saying a word to either Diana or Art.

"Just as well Charlotte paid us before she went," said Art.

"I wonder what happens next?" Diana mused.

"Oh they'll make it up. More's the pity. Sad to see a nice person like Charlotte waste time on a loser."

And that was that until a few months later. Diana was browsing the internet. She was looking for the meaning of names for a friend's baby daughter. She typed in Lily and the search came back with Lily the Ladybird.

'*New series of Lily the Ladybird by Charlotte L Cross.*' Diana clicked through the Amazon site on to the biopic. Alongside a beaming picture of Charlotte, it stated:

"*Award-winning writer Charlotte Cross has just launched a new series of Lily the Ladybird. Born in London, England Charlotte now lives full time in New Zealand where she works closely with schools and colleges. Her books are a great way for children to discover the delights of learning.*"

"So there is life after fifty," Diana smiled and raised her coffee mug in a toast. "Good for you Charlotte," she said.

Chapter Seven: Witness Protection

The doorbell rang.

"Ah they're here," said Diana.

She opened the door. "Welcome to Minefield."

"Good to be here. My name's Paul and this is my partner, Trevor.

Diana raised her eyebrows. They were a good looking pair in their late twenties/early thirties. Paul was clean shaven with a crew cut, blue eyes and brown hair. For Diana this was perfection on legs. He wore jeans and T-shirt with trainers and a leather jacket slung over his shoulder. Trevor was stockier but he clearly worked out. Muscles rippled everywhere. His arms were laced with a distinctive Celtic-style tattoo of curves and crescents.

"What a waste to womankind," she muttered to herself as she showed them into the room. "Paul was the talker. Trevor seemed more of the moody James Dean type," she reflected to Sue in one of those women-that-take-afternoon-tea gossips that I love listening to. Everyone knows that walls have ears!

"This is great," said Paul. "Thank you so much for putting us up at such short notice."

"We're delighted to have you," said Diana. "We don't have anyone booked so you can stay as long as you like."

"It will probably only be for three days until our friends get back," said Paul. "It's just one of those things. Family crisis and they had to run. Did you say we are the only people staying here?"

"Yes. We just have the one room at the front. You can come and go as you like. You won't be disturbed. Not by us anyway."

"Oh?" asked Paul.

"They're fundraising for the church," said Diana. "In this village that means harvest suppers, teddy bear parachuting from the church tower and open gardens. Everyone has got roped in. Somehow I've agreed to provide cream teas as part of the Open Garden event tomorrow. It's been advertised in the parish magazine. I've had three goes at making scones already. They come out like lead weights. I'm going to have to buy some."

Paul laughed. "You don't need to do that. Trevor is a dab hand with the scones. He can help you and I'll help with the teas. We need something to do to keep us occupied over the next few days, don't we Trevor?"

"Do we?" Trevor glared at him. In fact there seemed a lot of communication going on between the two of them but Diana didn't notice.

"Oh yes," said Paul. "Trevor has an NVQ3 don't you? He's had a lot of experience in catering for large numbers. It should be fun."

"Oh my goodness. That would be terrific." Diana was very quick to take them up on the offer. "Perhaps we could all start together after breakfast tomorrow. I'll go and buy some more ingredients. With all of us on the job we can do cheese, plain and fruit scones. Art, my husband, has accidentally on purpose chosen to go to a radio hams convention this weekend so I would so welcome any help I can get."

"We'll look forward to it," beamed Paul as he closed the door.

"Lucky f**king Art," said Trevor. "Is this your idea of a joke?"

"I'm sure I read that you worked in the kitchens during your last stay as her Majesty's guest."

Trevor was pacing round the room. "First of all you f**k up on the safe house. Then you tell me the plans have changed and we have to go underground. Then you bring me to a public house…."

"It's a private bed and breakfast."

"To a public house in the middle of a village with more twitching curtains than I've had hot dinners. You introduce me as your gay partner, put me in this pokey room and tell me we are going to be sleeping together."

"Not exactly …"

"And then you volunteer me to cook scones for the entire f**king village."

"Precisely," said Paul. "Hidden in full view. What else are you going to do? It's true the safe house was compromised. But just be grateful we found out before you ended up talking to the fishes wearing your concrete wellies."

There was silence as Trevor grudgingly processed this information.

"We should be further away from Felixstowe," he grumbled.

"Why? What difference does it make? Your '*friends*' are scattered across the country and, in particular, all the way up the A14 from Felixstowe to the Midlands."

"Who knows I'm here?"

"Only those that need to. The leak has been plugged. The trial has already started. There will be a new safe house on Monday. We'll move to Ipswich ready for you to give evidence on Tuesday. You'll be back to the original plan. New identify, new location, new life."

"You could have picked something with a different name," said Trevor. "Minefield. I feel like I'm tiptoeing between them."

"What do you expect? You should have stuck to the small time hustling. Just think yourself lucky, you're getting a second chance."

"A second chance? Looking over my shoulder for the rest of my life? Waiting for them to catch up with me? You've already shown your security is about as much use as a one legged man in an arse kicking competition."

Paul bowed and pointed to the door. "Your choice," he said.

Silence.

"Just to be clear. I'm no f**king poof," Trevor said.

"And I like the right hand side of the bed," he added. He got on it and turned the TV on, switching through the channels until he found some sports. "You might have found somewhere with Sky Sports!"

"You want jam on it?" said Paul.

I listened with interest when Diana turned the TV on that evening. It was Look East. The BBC reporter was standing on Ipswich Crown Court steps.

"James Brogue is one of five men charged with various counts of bringing illegal immigrants, drugs and other contraband into the country via Felixstowe port. Opening the case for the prosecution, Nigel Barrage QC said that this was a multi-million pound operation involving corruption and human trafficking on a scale hitherto unknown. All defendants plead 'Not Guilty'."

I felt very protective. Diana was here on her own. If I had put the pieces of the jigsaw together correctly then we had a key witness for this trial staying with us. He must have turned Queen's evidence to save his own skin. And he was being hunted by ruthless predators that placed no value on human life or decency. All that stood between them and us was this Paul character. The very person who had chosen to put Diana's life at risk. It was clear the operation had already been bodged once. How could I be sure that this was the only leak?

* * * * * * * * * *

The next day Paul, Trevor and Diana gathered in the kitchen.

"How many scones do you need to make?" asked Paul.

"I'm not sure. It's a lovely day. Charles said at least one hundred when I met him yesterday. He's making sure everyone pushes people this way."

"Who's Charles?" asked Trevor.

"Oh he's our parish clerk and lay preacher. He's coming over later with his partner Derek. They're bringing the chairs and tables from the village hall."

"Are there many queers here? .. I mean gays." asked Trevor.

Diana gave him a quizzical look. "I don't know. I've never counted. There are a few couples but round here it's no big deal."

"So … ouch!" Trevor rubbed his ankle.

"So …. there's no discrimination?" Paul jumped in. "It's just we get quite a bit where we live."

Diana smiled at him. "Don't worry. You're safe here. And you're certainly not the "only gays in the village". Minefielders get worked up about things that matter like windfarms on the airbase or who has queue jumped for a place in the chicken co-operative."

"You didn't have to kick me," hissed Trevor when Diana's back was turned.

"Then mind your f**king language," hissed back Paul.

Trevor was certainly an organised cook. He'd clearly picked up some skills from his time in prison kitchens and the hot scones began to skid off the trays.

"What a wonderful smell of baking." Charles' head poked through the fly curtains into the kitchen.

"No darlings." He raised an appreciative eyebrow when he saw Paul and Trevor. "Don't stop on my account. I'm just here to deliver the chairs. I see you've got some help anyway."

"Yes," said Diana. "Paul and Trevor meet our parish clerk, Charles. They are staying here for a few days and have kindly agreed to help with the cooking and serving, given your plans to direct the entire village through here."

"One needs to aim at the stars even if we only hit next door's dustbin," said Charles airily. "I don't suppose that one of you big strong lads would help me move the tables?"

"I think I'm needed in the kitchen," said Trevor. "Paul be a dear and help Charles out will you? You're much better at that sort of practical thing than I am."

"Terrific," said Charles. "Come along then Paul."

"What do you think you're playing at?" whispered Paul fiercely as he passed Trevor to go outside.

"Just getting into role." Trevor was grinning ear to ear. "Miss you already," he added as Paul went outside.

By 12 noon, when the gates opened, they were good to go. The weather remained fine and more people came through than we, at the Vicarage, had seen in years. It took me back to the old garden fêtes we used to hold. The children ran around in the garden, darting into the woodland areas, playing football in the field. I have to admit that Trevor and Paul were good. They really worked as a team serving tea, joining in with the small talk, clearing tables, washing up. It was hard to believe who they really were. They were the stars of the show and drew in more people than the scones.

At 6 pm the last of the stragglers left. Diana, Trevor and Paul collapsed on to the striped deckchairs on the patio just outside the kitchen.

"I'm whacked," said Trevor.

"You've both been absolutely brilliant," said Diana. "I don't know how I'd have managed without you. Your cloud turned out to be my silver lining."

"It's actually been really good fun," said Trevor. "It's nice to feel you've made a contribution."

Diana put the bag of money on the table. "I reckon there's about £300 here for the church."

Right on cue, Charles came round the corner. "Coo-ee," he said. "It's only me darlings. Didn't you do well? The scones are the talk of the village as indeed are you two. The gallant knights who rescued a fair damsel in distress. I'm not stopping. I've just come to collect the money. We can catch up more tomorrow night at the bridge evening. There'll also be a bit of supper. Nothing too grand. It's a Greek theme and Derek does an amazing meze." He picked up the money bag and rushed off to his next port of call.

"Bridge?" Trevor looked directly at Paul who, in turn, avoided eye contact.

"Oh, yes. Did I forget to tell you? Charles invited us. We've not doing anything tomorrow night so I thought we might as well. Might be fun. Meet some kindred spirits."

"You are honoured," said Diana. "It's a very select few that get to go to the bridge nights. Derek's cooking is legendary."

"You've never gone?"

"No. I think it's just for special friends."

"You mean other gays? You've got a gay club in Minefield?" Trevor asked.

Diana considered this. "Well I suppose when you put it like that … yes we have. I didn't see it in that way before." She got up. "Well I'll leave you hallowed creatures to bask in the sunshine of your success," she said. "Us lesser mortals have got a battlefield in the kitchen to sort out."

"Just shoot the casualties," laughed Paul. "They give fewer problems."

Trevor waited until Diana was out of earshot before he exploded.

"My last night of freedom and you're taking me to play bridge with a bunch of gays? Bridge!!"

"It's a game of cards, like whist."

"I know what it f**king is! Well I'm not going." He sounded a bit petulant.

"What else are you going to do? It's not much of a risk. No one would look for you there."

Silence.

"Greek meze sounds good," Paul said.

"How do we know what they get up to? If anyone touches me, bones will break."

"It's bridge. It's not an orgy."

"I was supposed to go out in a blaze of glory: high speed car chases, gun battles, coked up to the eyeballs, probably a helicopter or two. What do I get? Bridge night! What have you got planned for tomorrow afternoon? Knitting circles with the over seventies club? Are we going to church too? Perhaps we can rent an allotment space."

"You can't. They're all taken. Joe told me."

"Who the f**k is Joe?" Trevor was incredulous.

"You know. The old boy. He looks a hundred but he's clearly fit as a fiddle. The gardener."

"Is this a joke? Have we just walked into the twilight zone? We don't live here. I'm an international drugs trafficker and you're a cop. Remember?"

"Still nice to be part of a community don't you think?" said Paul.

Silence.

"Greek?" said Trevor.

"Legendary cook," said Paul.

Silence.

"Alright. You win. There's one other thing," said Trevor.

"What?"

"I can't remember the rules of bridge."

* * * * * * * * * *

The next day was very hot again. The pair helped Diana clear away tables and chairs. They set off for bridge around 7 pm.

Paul had a whole set of pay as you go SIM cards which he changed regularly, presumably to stop anyone tracing them through the phone network. Before they left for the 'gay club', as Trevor insisted on calling it, Paul went into the meadow to make his nightly call to the team. As usual I listened in. It didn't sound good.

"You think there is another leak? What do they know? Where is it coming from? It must be somewhere high up the food chain? Yes ... agreed or someone who could have access to the files. Do I stay or go? How safe is this new place going to be if we can't find the leak? You're sure no one else knows where we are? Just you and me. Not even the Chief at the moment? We're off the official radar? So we're OK to stay? We'll come straight to the court tomorrow. Let me know if anything changes. You can get me tonight on this number. Oh and do us a favour? Find the bloody squealer." Paul shut off the phone. He closed his eyes and seemed to be breathing deeply.

I got a sense of how scared he was. He was putting Diana at risk but if looked to me as if he was also being hung out to dry. There were people with a vested interest in James Brogue's acquittal. If they got wind of where Paul and Trevor were hiding there might be a blood bath. I had seen the gun Paul carried. A 9 mm Grandpower K100, Slovak semi-automatic pistol. This was serious and deadly.

A vicarage has certain emergency powers. But they should only be used in extremis and to protect the residents of the parish. I thought this was one such case and luckily the powers weren't removed when I was de-frocked. At 8 pm I shut off all airborne signals to Minefield. Mobile phones within the village and for a mile surrounding it were now completely useless.

Paul and Trevor came back around 11.30 pm. It had clearly been a good evening.

"What a great bunch of people. My God that man can cook," Trevor was saying as they came up the drive. "I don't think I'll need to eat for a week. Perhaps that's what I should do in my new life. A bit of outside catering. Film sets perhaps. Catering to the stars."

"In your dreams!! I'd say you had over indulged in the Ouzo." Paul was checking his phone. "That's funny, no signal."

"Simply responding to the hospitality of the hosts," chirruped Trevor.

"Keep your voice down. You'll wake Diana. It's an early start tomorrow. I told her no breakfast, so we'll be on our way by 7 am."

"No breakfast? 7 am? Middle of the night."

Trevor fell on the bed and was snoring within five minutes. Paul checked the room still trying for a phone signal. Eventually he gave up and sat down, evidently intending to keep vigil. Within half an hour he was asleep too.

Between midnight and 5.30 am the Old Vicarage disappeared. Helped by the absence of street lighting and a cloudy night, I made the house invisible. The driveway and garden looked like an extension of the allotments across the road.

Around 4 am, a Range Rover drove slowly up the road and then back again. It did this two or three times, finally stopping outside the caravan park. Luckily our postcode on satellite navigation systems covers about half a square mile and a number of properties including a certificated caravan site, where up to five caravans can park at any time. Visitors were always getting muddled.

Two figures, both dressed in black, got out and looked round.

"This can't be it. He said a bed and breakfast."

"Phone him and double check. We don't want a bloodbath here." A distinct Black Country accent floated through the stillness of the night.

"No f**king signal. Are we even in the right village? F**king rural backwater."

The silence was disturbed by the sound of a dog barking, followed by the crowing of a cockerel. Dawn was beginning to break.

"Morning," a disembodied voice came out of the gloom. Joe and his dog, Munch, took shape.

"Can I help you gents?" he said.

"We're looking for a bed and breakfast," said Black Country. "We were told there is one around here."

Joe scratched his chin. "Well there's the pub up the road," he said slowly.

"Not the pub. Somewhere else in the village. On Sanctuary Lane we were told."

"Well .." Joe looked puzzled. I've been living here for 10 years and I've never heard of it. There's Dunroamin' in Lymestead. That's the next village along."

"No that won't be it. We were looking for one around here." Black Country's colleague spoke impatiently.

"Nope. Never heard of it. Just the pub. Bit early ain't it for breakfast? Bit late for bed." Joe chuckled to himself as if pleased with his little joke.

"Well thanks anyway," said Black Country and got back into the Range Rover.

"Ah well … oh hang on a minute … I've just thought."

"Yes?"

Joe paused for a moment and scratched his chin again. "No. It's gone. Come along Munch. Be seeing you gents." He wandered off.

"Shall we shoot him anyway? Stupid arsehole." Black Country muttered.

They heard a rumbling, looked up and saw a tractor heading towards them.

"I give up," said Black Country. "It's like Piccadilly Circus round here."

They got back in the Range Rover and drove off.

Joe watched them go. "Something is rotten in the state of Denmark, Munch," he said. "It can stay in Denmark."

Paul woke from a deep sleep at 6 am and started as he realised where he was. He looked out of the window and then at Trevor who was still snoring. The sunlight was pouring in. He got up, stretched and reached for his mobile phone. He noticed there was a signal. He also noticed the text icon was flashing. "Ring me. Urgent. James." he read.

Paul changed the SIM card and rang the normal number. The call was picked up immediately.

"Is that you Paul? Are you OK?"

Paul recognised the voice and was surprised.

"Morning Chief. Yes fine."

"It was DC James Bowles who was the leak."

"But I spoke to him yesterday. He's sent me a text asking me to call him."

"There's no time to explain. He must have been laying a trap."

"How did you find out?"

"We've had our suspicions for some time. We've been monitoring his calls. There was one this morning about 5 am from a rather well known Black Country mobster. Something about directions to Minefield and an ancient looking village idiot."

"Well it's all quiet here, Chief. The witness is snoring his head off at the moment. We'll see you later."

* * * * * * * * *

That evening Art came back from his Ham Radio Amateurs conference.

"How did the garden event go?" he asked a little sheepishly.

"Oh fine," said Diana. "I had two really lovely B&B guests who helped me out. We raised £347 for the church."

"Oh good," said Art. "That was lucky. There weren't any other problems?"

"Nope," said Diana. "Everything was quiet and peaceful. But if you ever leave me in the lurch like that again, I won't be responsible for my actions."

Art was on his own with that one. I can divert the wrath of international drug runners but even my powers can't calm a good woman when she's riled.

Chapter Eight: Family Units

Peter had been staying at the Old Vicarage B&B on and off for over a year. He came once every six weeks or so and stayed for the weekend. He lived in Aberdeen and worked offshore, so it was a big trek down here to Suffolk.

The attraction was his two children. Tessa was eight and Peter Jnr was twelve. The separation with his wife, Christine, had been very bitter. It was a common enough story. A wife who felt herself neglected and had fallen for the first man to show her some attention. That relationship had not lasted but she met someone else through internet dating and they had moved into a rented cottage in Minefield. Christine was naturally discontented and carried her unhappiness with her. The present relationship seemed as doomed as any other.

Peter liked staying with us. It meant the children had somewhere to come and play. So he was more than just a McDonald's Dad. It was a joy to hear them kicking a ball around my garden, climbing my trees in the orchard or picking blackberries together.

As Diana and Art got to know and trust Peter they let him use more of the house. So he would cook with the children in the kitchen and they would all eat together. He was a gruff man with a clipped Scottish accent and few words but he had a heart of gold and clearly adored the children.

"He's no charmer though," Diana said to Art. "If Christine wanted wining, dining and flattery she'd have been looking in the wrong place with Peter."

"He's an honest man and a good provider," said Art.

"It's not always enough, I'm afraid," said Diana.

It was a weekend in March when things came to a head. Peter arrived, as usual, late on Friday evening having flown down from Aberdeen to Norwich and picked up a hire car.

"We're going to Ipswich tomorrow," he said to Diana and Art. "Although it pains me, Peter Jnr has become an Ipswich Town supporter and there's a local derby. I've got tickets for us all."

"That won't have been cheap," said Art. "Not if you add everything up."

"It'll be worth it to see the lad's face," said Peter.

He asked for an early breakfast so he could pick up the children in good time. But thirty minutes later he was back.

He came into the kitchen where Art and Diana were washing up. "She won't let me in," said Peter pacing the kitchen floor.

"Why not?" asked Art.

"She said it wasn't convenient and they weren't at my beck and call. Then she said the child maintenance wasn't enough to cover all the bills and if I wanted to see the kids I would have to provide more. I said I'd got tickets for the local derby and she said that proved the point. If I had enough money for that kind of treat when she couldn't even put food on the table then I could afford to pay more."

He looked at them both.

"But I already give them over 50% of what I have. There was some overtime available so I grabbed it to pay for the tickets. I don't know how I could find anymore."

Diana could see Peter was getting wound up. "You don't need to justify yourself to us. We know you're doing your best."

"So what happened?" asked Art.

"Well nothing. She just shouted at me and slammed the door in my face. I was so shocked I didn't say anything. I just walked off."

"I have a rule when Diana gets into a temper," said Art.

Diana raised her eyebrows and gave him a look. He was obviously prepared to live dangerously and ignored her.

"It's called the 40 minute rule. You leave things for 40 minutes and then you go back. You apologise even if it's not your fault. You take the flack and then it all calms down."

Peter seemed dubious. "It never worked when we were married. Once Chrissy got a strop that was it for days." He glanced at Diana. "Does it work?"

"Art thinks it does!" she said. "Perhaps she's had a bad night or the kids have been playing up and she just wants to explode at someone."

"She's got her new partner, David, for that now," said Peter. "I lost the part of verbal punch bag when she left me."

"Well I do recognise when I've been a bit unreasonable and flown off the handle at someone," said Diana. "But knowing and backing down are two different things. You need to find a way to let her back down with dignity."

"Women. I'll never understand them," said Peter.

"We're not supposed to," said Art. "It's part of their charm."

Peter considered all this. "OK. I'll give it a bit and phone. But the clock is ticking. We need to get down to Ipswich or we'll miss the match."

Half an hour later they heard Peter make the call. He was in his room but the sound of his raised and increasingly frustrated voice came floating through into the kitchen.

"Well I'm coming now, so have the kids ready." They heard the front door slam as Peter marched down the drive.

Art looked at Diana. "I don't think it's going well."

"As agony aunts, we make good ditch diggers," she said.

Two hours later the front door slammed again.

Diana and Art had gone out so it was just Peter and me … and what looked like a 1 litre bottle of whisky.

Peter spent the afternoon in front of the television. By evening the bottle was half empty. During the course of the afternoon he had left a number of texts and messages on Christine's phone. They were becoming increasingly incoherent. "You're a great mother," he slurred. "Let me be a great dad." Luckily by 6 pm he'd fallen asleep in a drunken stupor.

* * * * * * * * *

"Christine was in the village shop and the kids were in the car." Diana was in the kitchen preparing tea. Art had the job of chopping the onions and the tears were streaming down his face.

"Try a spoon in your mouth," she said.

"Doesn't work. Go on .... What did Christine say?"

"Well .. I'm pretty sure she wanted to pretend she didn't recognise me, but it's a bit difficult in a shop that size especially as I said 'hello Christine'.

"I said: Peter's staying with us. He had some tickets for the Ipswich match. I bet Peter Jnr and Tessa were excited. She looked at me as if she wanted to stick pins in me and said: 'Well it's a pity he didn't bother to let us know. We had other things arranged. Excuse me.' And then she walked out. She put down her shopping and just left."

"So where's our guest?" asked Art.

"He must be in his room. I'm sure I heard the TV. Should we check on him?"

"No leave it. If he wants us, he'll come and find us."

* * * * * * * * * *

The next day was one of those bright and breezy March days when the wind has dropped a bit, the skies are bright blue and the sun is warm. A teaser for the Spring. Humans get excited about these days but houses do too. I loved to feel the warmth on my roof tiles.

When Peter didn't appear for breakfast, Art knocked on the bedroom door. It wasn't locked so he tentatively pushed it open.

"He's gone," he reported to Diana. "His clothes are strewn over the floor and his car's outside but he's not in his room."

"Unlike Peter to miss his breakfast."

"There's something else. His bed looks as if it's not been slept in, just lain on and there's this." Art held up the empty whisky bottle.

"Perhaps he got completely smashed yesterday and has gone out for a walk to get rid of the hang over," suggested Diana.

"Hm ..Yes may be. Probably a bit early to worry."

But I'd seen what Diana and Art hadn't and I was worried. Peter had woken up about 9 pm, drunk the rest of the bottle and left the house two hours later. He hadn't come back that night and he didn't come back at all that Sunday.

Art tried his mobile but it went to answerphone.

"Do you think we should call someone?" said Art.

"Who?" said Diana.

"The police?"

"He's a grown male. The police won't be interested – it's only been a few hours."

"Christine, then?"

"I'm not sure either Christine or Peter will thank us for interfering. Let's leave it a couple of hours. He might just be licking his wounds. If he hasn't come back then we'll try his mobile again."

"When was he going back to Scotland?"

"He's due to leave on Tuesday. If we don't see him before tomorrow night we'll call Christine and then, if needs be, the police."

* * * * * * * * *

Weekends are always allotment days. A string of people come from all over the village and beyond to tend to their gardens. Of course this is no ordinary space. There is much competition between the gardeners. At times the variety of fruit, vegetables and flowers would look well exhibited at the Chelsea Flower Show. The allotments are also a place where you get the most amazing, and often, fantastical bits of gossip. Very useful for a vicarage with responsibility for the village.

That Sunday I was tuning into the talk and realised that it was about Christine and her family.

"I gather that David walked out." Bert, the tree warden, said to Joe as they looked at the chickens. "Leastways, his car has been gone for a few weeks now. Jane told Mildred in the shop she was worried about them kids. She shouts something awful at them. Especially the boy."

"Last time I was in there I heard Christine asking if the shop offers credit. Mind you she's a grumpy shrew for all she's not bad looking."

"Hmm," said Bert. He changed the subject. "So how's the latest arrival coming on?"

"See for yourself. She's going to be a good layer." And they were back to talk of chickens, lay levels and the best feed.

So Christine's partner had left. That explained the anxiety about money, the stress and maybe the bitterness towards Peter. Whichever way you looked, it was an unhappy mess. One I had seen all too often. Couples setting out with hope who found themselves by degrees hating and hurting each other.

Art tried Peter's number again and again. Nothing.

"I'm getting really worried," he said.

"OK. Let's give it until Monday lunchtime. If you haven't heard anything, call Christine and then the police. I'm in court tomorrow. I'll call you at lunchtime so you can give me an update."

"Right oh. I'll hold off until then."

Diana was a magistrate and her court duties took about a day each month. Normally, to tie in with work and other commitments, she did Mondays. Mondays were trial days: usually hearing not guilty pleas for minor assaults, criminal damage or motoring matters. It also meant dealing with people who had been arrested over the weekend and were remanded in cells. She enjoyed the work. "It's the stories behind the crimes that make it so interesting," she would say. "Even when you see the same offence – like drunk driving - over and over again, the story is different."

She called Art at lunchtime as promised.

"You can call off the search for Peter," she said. "He's here."

"In court?" Art was incredulous.

"Yes he was in the cells over the weekend and he appeared before us today. It was quite a shock. I had no idea. I had to declare an interest so I sat to one side while they dealt with the case."

"But why was he there?"

"The police picked him up late Saturday night/early Sunday morning. Apparently he went round to Christine's. He was drunk. He's been charged with criminal damage and common assault."

"He hit her?"

"I'm not sure if there was any physical contact but she's saying he threatened her and pushed her around. Peter pleaded guilty to the CD but not guilty to the common assault."

"Will there be a trial?"

"Yes but obviously I won't be involved."

"So where is he now?"

"He was given conditional bail. He's not to contact Christine or the children while he's on bail and he's not to come into Suffolk except to see his solicitor or attend court. The only exception is that he can come and collect his stuff from us, but he's got to be out of Suffolk by 5 pm this afternoon. I wanted to let you know he's on his way."

"Poor Peter," said Art. "You can't help but feel sorry for him. He's been led a fine old dance. I'm sure he wouldn't touch a hair on anyone's head."

"You never know what people will do when they are cornered. Add to that a bottle of whisky. One explosive cocktail, ready to serve. I'm not saying there wasn't provocation or there won't be mitigation but it's not looking good for him. And, of course, now he's lost the very thing that he's been trying to keep – the contact with Tessa and Peter Jnr. Anyway. Got to go. I'm due back in court at 2 pm and there's some papers to read."

Art put the phone down. "Bloody women. They pull our strings and we dance to their tune," he grumbled.

An hour later Peter arrived in a taxi.

"I suppose you've heard," he said to Art. "I didn't know Diana was a magistrate."

"It was a shock for her too," said Art.

"I'll just get my stuff and go," said Peter.

"Why don't you have a shower first, mate? I'll make you a sandwich. It's been a pretty shitty weekend."

Peter stared at him. There were tears in his eyes and he brushed them away angrily as they began to roll down his cheeks. The prickly defensiveness was gone. He just looked wounded and bewildered. The planned happiness of the weekend had been smashed to pieces.

"Yeah. Maybe I will."

A pause.

"Thanks."

Half an hour later, over a cheese and pickle sandwich Peter reflected on the carnage of the weekend.

"Chrissie's always been able to push my buttons," he said. "When I went round the second time, it was clear she'd taken the kids out. The car wasn't in the drive. So I went for a walk and came back hoping they'd be in. I kept trying to ring her mobile but it just went to answerphone and she didn't respond to my texts. I just got angrier and angrier. I didn't know where they'd gone. So in the end I went to the shop and bought a bottle of whisky."

"We found it," said Art. "You drank the whole bottle?"

"I remember lying on the bed, watching TV. I kept making phone calls but she still didn't pick up. Eventually I must have fallen asleep. When I woke up I had a splitting headache. There was still some whisky in the bottle. I just finished it off. From then on everything feels a bit muddled but I know I got more and more cross. There was a film on about a bloke losing contact with his family and having to start again. I just didn't want that to be me. So about 11 pm I went back to find them."

"11 pm?" Art raised his eyebrows. "Wouldn't the kids have been in bed?"

"I wasn't thinking straight. Anyway I remember falling over the gate. I think I broke it off the hinges. There's a heck of a bruise on my leg. And I banged on the door and was calling out for Chrissie to open it. Eventually she opened the window and told me to go away. She said I was frightening the children. I said I wouldn't go until she came down and talked to me. She then said she'd call the police. I remember pleading with her just to talk with me. The lights started to come on in some of the neighbouring houses and she said she'd come downstairs if I'd go away. She opened the door but must have changed her mind because she then tried to close it. I put my hand out to stop her closing the door and tripped over the front door step. The force of the closing door must have pushed me backwards because I remember falling over and banging my head. I just lay there looking at the stars for a long time and the next thing I knew the police had arrived. They carted me off and the rest you probably know. But I didn't touch her. I don't know why she says I did."

"Revenge?" suggested Art. "Although it sounds like you were blotto. Are you sure you remember everything?"

"I know I'm a big bloke and maybees I'm a bit rough in my manner. But there are limits. I'd never hurt a woman."

"Well whatever happened, that was one expensive bottle of whisky," said Art.

"It's cost me everything. I may never see the kids again. I can't even talk to them. What am I going to do?" Peter buried his head in his hands.

"I don't know," said Art. "But I do know something from what Diana tells me. Once you are in the court system, don't try and beat it…Don't break your bail conditions. Follow the rules."

"You don't think I should try and call them?"

"I'm sorry mate. From where I'm standing all the cards are stacked against you. Anything you do now will count against you. What if you call and Christine reports it? She could get a restraining order. Where children are concerned, it's a woman's world. Even now. You and Christine need some breathing space."

Peter looked interested. "You sound like you are speaking from experience?"

Art chose to ignore him. "The first rule is that you need to be out of Suffolk by 5 pm," he said looking at his watch. "I'll get your bag."

When Diana arrived home a couple of hours later, she found Art staring at a cold cup of tea. "Everything OK?" she asked.

"Yes. Peter's gone," he said.

She looked at him. "How about you?"

"Fine. Just stirred up some old memories I'd rather forget."

"It's not the same, you know. Nothing like."

"It's still the same system. Interfering. Taking the woman's side."

Diana was quiet for a moment. She ruffled his hair. "I'll make us another cup of tea," she said.

* * * * * * * * *

We never saw Peter again. Christine moved away from the village soon after. So I don't know how it ended. But we weren't very hopeful.

I suppose that's one of the differences between the world of a vicarage and that of a bed and breakfast. Now I only get to see segments of lives. Those lives go on for better or worse long after we've played our part. Peter's story wasn't particularly unique but that didn't make it the less sad. Sometimes you just can't fix everything.

Chapter Nine: Ruby Anniversary

Diana had overslept. She stumbled out of bed, hobbled to the bathroom, dropped the mouthwash on the floor and hit her head on the sink as she picked it up. She slung on the first clothes she could find and tore outside to let out the chickens who were squawking loudly in protest at being denied access to the garden and their usual patrol. She walked backwards and forwards to the house three times in the process. First she forgot to get the grain to feed them out of the greenhouse. Then she forgot to shut the greenhouse door and finally she forgot the key to her garden office. She made a mug of coffee using an old Tassimo coffee tablet and then dropped the mug and broke it as she spat the muddy flavourless water out. This was not going to be a good day.

Art had gone to the shops. Diana worked full time during the week so she had a lie in on Saturdays. But today she had things she wanted to do and hadn't intended to sleep so late.

The doorbell rang.

"Oh blast," said Diana who was on her knees collecting the broken china and mopping up the mess she had made. She went to the door and realised it was locked and she couldn't find the key.

"Sorry," she called through the letterbox. I'll be with you in a moment. I'm just trying to find the key. It took her what seemed like an age but finally she located it under some paperwork on the radiator cover in the hall. She opened the door.

A smartly dressed couple in their early seventies smiled at her. Diana passed her hand automatically through her unbrushed hair. She looked down and realised she was wearing her shirt inside out. Unfortunately the curry stain down the front was still showing through. He baggy tracksuit bottoms also had a huge grass stain on the leg.

"I'm so sorry," she began. "I know I look a mess. I overslept. It was one of those really deep sleeps where you wake up not knowing who you are and basically it just went downhill from there ..." she trailed off.

"Don't apologise, we're sorry to have disturbed you." The lady had a beautiful face with deep blue twinkly eyes that belied her real age. Her white silky hair was pinned in a bun at the back of her head. She wore a pleated skirt and a matching jacket.

"My name is Rose Sadler and this is my husband, Gerard."

Gerard was equally elegant. He was tall and slim with a full head of grey hair. He wore a tie and there was some kind of insignia on his blue blazer. He stared sternly at her.

"Young lady, your shirt is inside out and there is a stain on it."

Diana blushed. "Yes I'm really sorry."

"How can we expect guests to believe we offer a five star service when we greet them looking as if we have fallen through a hedge backwards?"

Diana stammered out her reply. "No, you're quite right. It gives the wrong impression."

"It certainly does. I hope other standards haven't slipped. I shall want to see you in my office at 15:30 so we can take a look at all aspects of service: bar, restaurant, laundry, housekeeping, maintenance ... I shall want to see all the usual performance indicators. In fact bring all the department managers if they can be released from their duties."

Diana was now completely nonplussed. Rose stepped in. "Now Gerard. We're on holiday, remember. You're not at work today."

She turned to Diana. "Gerard used to be general manager of a chain of hotels. He sometimes forgets where he is and goes back in time a bit, don't you Gerard?"

Gerard wasn't listening. He had started to walk along the front of the Vicarage. He had taken out a notebook and pen and was busy making notes. The words 'smeared windows' came floating across the drive.

Meantime Art drove in, parked and got out with the groceries.

"Morning," he said cheerfully.

"Ah, young man," said Gerard. "And who does your outside maintenance?"

"That'll be me," said Art. "I do kitchens, laundry, gardening, rickshaw driving … you name it."

Gerard looked in horror at him. "Well no wonder everything's going to pot. We need to get you some help my boy. Look at the moss on this drive? I have called a manager's meeting this afternoon. This place has potential. We'll soon get things back on track."

Art didn't miss a beat. "That would be great, Mr er .."

"Sadler .. Gerard Sadler." Gerard beamed at Art. "I can see we are going to get along," he said.

Rose turned back to Diana. "We are looking to stay in Minefield for a couple of nights and wondered if you could put us up?"

Diana looked a little uncertain. "Of course we can," said Art.

"Why doesn't Diana show Mrs Sadler to the room? I'll take Mr Sadler round to the patio and I'll make some coffee for all of us. It's a lovely day. There might even be some cake."

Rose looked relieved. "That would be lovely."

Half an hour later they sat together on the patio. Diana had brushed her hair, put on a blouse and a pair of trousers. Gerard nodded approvingly. "That's better," he said. He still had his notebook and was making notes as he looked round the garden.

"Do you want to inspect all the grounds, Mr Sadler?" asked Art. "I can show you round, if you like."

"Splendid idea," said Gerard. "I'll take my coffee with me. I hope you'll excuse me ladies. Business calls."

Rose smiled and waved them off.

"Your husband is very kind," she said. "I suppose the fact this is a bed and breakfast has triggered Gerard's old memories. He was fine this morning."

"Will he come forward in time, later on?" asked Diana.

"I don't know," said Rose. "It's such an adventure with Gerard. He takes us to some wonderful places with that imagination."

She sipped her coffee.

"So what brings you to Minefield?" asked Diana.

"It's our fortieth wedding anniversary tomorrow," said Rose. "We got married in Minefield church. In fact the room we are staying in now is the one where we talked through our plans for the wedding with the vicar and had our marriage classes."

"Oh how wonderful." Diana was really moved. "So you are from Minefield?"

"Well I am, although we were both over thirty when we married. I had moved away. I was working as a nursing sister in a hospital in Brighton. That's how we met. Gerard was a keen cricketer. Always has been. He broke his thumb during a match and came into the accident and emergency department still wearing his cricket whites. He looked so dashing. It was love at first sight. At thirty I thought marriage had passed me by and I was quite happy with my career. I was knocked for six. Bowled over you might say. He still insisted on asking my parent's permission to marry me despite our advanced ages. We had many happy visits here both before and after."

She sighed.

"But Gerard doesn't seem to remember that period."

"So you were hoping to jog his memory by coming here?" Diana asked.

"That's about the sum of it." Rose smiled warmly at her. "Fingers crossed!" she said.

"Will you have family coming to help you celebrate?" asked Diana.

"No – it's just Gerard and me. We weren't blessed with children. But we've had an amazing life together and I can't think of anyone else I'd rather be with."

* * * * * * * * *

"It must be so hard for Rose," said Diana later. "Not knowing from one day to the next if you are sharing memories with your life partner or a stranger. What a terrible disease dementia is."

"The long goodbye," agreed Art. "My grandfather had it. But I think there were some compensations. He went to places and saw and said things that just gave a different way of thinking about life – especially in the early phases of his illness.

"When I see one of those amazing sunsets when the sky is golden and fiery red I sometimes think of Grandad Alex. You know the night and the blackness is coming but while the sun is setting there is this magical bridge. I remember he used to go back to the war games he must have played as a child or perhaps it was his national service time. We marched about and took cover under haystacks when the enemy was attacking. My gran must have been pulling her hair out. But to me and my brother it was just a big game."

"You've never talked much about him before," said Diana

"Well he died when I was quite young and then the label of dementia wasn't one that people used easily. There was quite a stigma attached to it. I guess seeing Gerard has just pressed a few time travel buttons."

"What happened to your grandad in the end?"

"He shot himself," said Art.

"What .. by accident? As part of the war game memories?" asked Diana.

"No. I don't think so. From what I can gather and, even now, Dad won't talk about it … he had some awareness that he was losing his marbles and decided to end it early. It's not just about your mind wandering occasionally. Your body can start to shut down. You become incontinent. You forget how to eat, even to swallow. Maybe he had a lucid moment and could see it coming."

"How did your gran feel I wonder?"

"Heartbroken. He was her life. She only lived a year or so longer."

"Can you die of a broken heart?"

"I think you can. Officially it was cancer but I think the mind operates the body's defences. She just gave up and let the enemy in."

They both fell silent.

Diana spoke first.

"Rose talked about new adventures too. Perhaps she is determined to enjoy the sunset before night sets in… I'm going to bed. Coming?"

"In a bit," said Art. But it was several hours before he finally pulled off his headphones, turned off the music and went upstairs.

* * * * * * * * * *

The next day at breakfast, Rose was full of how they planned to spend the day.

"We'll walk up to the church," she said. "And then round the village. I see the pub is still open. It's cream teas rather than beer but no matter. We'll call in and see Mildred. We still keep in touch. She was my primary school teacher you know. It will be a lovely way to spend a wedding anniversary won't it Gerard?"

"Whose wedding anniversary?" asked Gerard.

"Ours silly. It's forty years to the day that we got married here in Minefield."

Gerard appeared to consider this. "Forty years… Minefield." He rolled the word round and smiled at his wife.

Art appeared from the kitchen. "Can I get you anything else?" he asked

Gerard picked up a napkin. "These are paper and only two-ply. You should be using the linen. We really need to get some of the basics sorted."

"Right you are, Mr Sadler," said Art. "But I don't want to interfere with your day off, so are you happy to leave this until later?"

Gerard considered this. "Fair enough," he said. "But I'll be back later to talk about arrangements for the anniversary celebration. We have a 40th anniversary coming up. It should be in the diary. Very important day." He looked at Rose. "That reminds me, our anniversary should be coming up soon."

"It certainly is," she said. "It's today."

Gerard looked puzzled. "So there are two anniversaries to celebrate," he said looking round the small dining room. "Well I don't know where everyone is going to sit."

"Don't worry," said Art. "I've got it covered."

"Shall we go for our walk, then?" asked Rose gently "And leave them to it?"

"Yes it's time I made a move too," said Art.

"Why?" asked Gerard. "Where are you going?"

* * * * * * * * *

Rose and Gerard spent the rest of the morning meandering round the village and visiting old friends. They came back around 2 pm.

"How did it go?" asked Diana who met them coming in.

"We had a lovely walk, didn't we Gerard?" said Rose.

"Yes, we did," said Gerard. "Lovely little village this but bit out of the way. Not much traffic. Not the best place to site a new hotel. I wonder why they've chosen it?"

Diana raised her eyebrows and looked at Rose. She shook her head softly and shrugged her shoulders.

"Gerard's a bit tired," she said. "We thought we'd have an afternoon nap before we go into Hassham later on."

Diana went into the kitchen. "It doesn't look like anything has jogged his memory," she reported to Art. "What a shame."

An hour later there was a knock at the kitchen window.

Art was peeling some apples to go with the blackberries he had picked earlier in the day. Even though it was only mid September the long hot summer had brought everything forward a month. It had been a fabulous year for fruit and the hedges were garlanded with red berries.

He looked up and saw Gerard.

"Hello Mr Sadler," he said going outside.

"Art," said Gerard. "I need your help and we are going to have to act quickly. As you know it's our fortieth wedding anniversary today and we got married in Minefield Church from this very vicarage. Rose is asleep so I want to get everything organised before she wakes up. Are you up for the challenge?"

Art beamed. "I'm at your disposal," he said.

Gerard got out his diary. It had a smart black leather cover and there were lots of useful pockets which provided some kind of filing system. He opened it and Art noticed the entries were beautifully neat and colour coded. But it all looked like hieroglyphics to him.

"I can't make head or tail of these entries," he said.

"No – it's a code. A sort of shorthand language I've built up over the years," said Gerard. "It has served me well. All my ideas on improvements and innovations to our services are stored here. I introduced the idea of weekend experiences: the hot air balloon ride, the golf pro weekend, the rally car experience. It's all commonplace now but it was quite innovative at the time. And I was big on employee participation and reward. Everyone needs to feel they are part of the team. Anyway the coding has become something of a habit and I still use it."

He found the page he was looking for.

"Now," he said. The Morgan should be arriving about 4pm. I'll drive us to St Joseph's and we'll get a taxi back so I can have a drink. Do you know St Joseph's?"

"The moated place? The one that's built on the remains of an old priory?" said Art.

"That's the one."

"Do I ever. Diana adores it. From what I remember the restaurant is set out in the main hall. It would have been the monks' chapter house."

"I've booked the whole room so we won't be disturbed," said Gerard consulting his notes. "The room has a gothic feel I believe with arched windows, wood panelling and stone floor. So I've asked that it be lit only by candles which should add to the atmosphere. I've arranged for a number of flowers which should cascade from the window sills and walls and these will largely be in white. But what I really want is forty red roses. One for each year of our marriage. I know it's short notice but do you know where I can get some? I was going to do it the other day but for some reason I haven't. I seem to have lost a couple of days and I haven't a clue where they went."

"There's a florist in Hassham. But I'll need to get a move on or they'll be shut," said Art. "I'll give them a call."

"I've also ordered a cake," said Gerard "But I'd really like to get some of those sparkler candles so it can be brought in with a bit of a flourish. You can get some quite dramatic ones. Do you know what I mean?"

"I know just the place," said Art who was beginning to get quite excited too. "How about the food? And do you have a special song you will be playing?"

"We're having Beef Wellington," said Gerard. "It's what we had at our wedding reception. And I've booked a quartet. They call themselves 'Locum'. They play a lot of swing – 1940s music – which is Rose's favourite. So we might have a bit of a dance too."

Art caught sight of Diana at the door. Her eyes were full of tears. She shook her head at him and moved away as if afraid that her presence might somehow disturb Gerard's thought processes.

Art got up to put things in motion. "Hang on .. what are you going to wear?" he asked.

Gerard consulted his book. "All in order," he said. The clothes will be arriving with the car. An evening suit. High collar and tails for me and a new dress for Rose."

Art was dubious. "You're a brave man," he said. "I wouldn't have a clue what to buy for Diana."

Gerard laughed. "I thought of that. I've put in one of her favourite dresses, just in case, and she brought something with her anyway."

He snapped his diary shut. "I think we've done. Are you OK to help?"

"Operation Ruby is Go," said Art.

* * * * * * * * *

The bright red Morgan sports car arrived at 4 pm. Art and Gerard lost twenty minutes drooling over it. "I used to race these as a hobby," said Gerard affectionately. "Rose and I drove a Morgan – a three-wheeler in racing green - across France one beautiful summer in the 1980s. I hope she hasn't forgotten."

Rose slept through until about 5 pm. When she woke it took a few seconds for her eyes to adjust and she had to blink a few times and pinch herself to check she wasn't still dreaming. The bucket of ice with champagne on the table, the red Morgan parked just outside the window and an evening suit hanging from the wardrobe. But her eyes were drawn mostly to the elegant cream evening dress with tiny jewels, sewn into the fabric, glinting in the sunlight.

"Hello, sleepy head," said Gerard. "Champagne's getting cold. Table's booked for 7.30 pm. Time to get in gear."

Two hours later Art and Diana waved them off.

"She looked sensational," said Diana.

"They both did," returned Art squeezing her hand. "Fancy a walk? We could pick some blackberries?"

"You smooth talker," Diana grinned.

* * * * * * * * *

Rose was first in to breakfast the next morning.

"Gerard's on his way," she said.

"How was it?" asked Diana.

"Unbelievable," said Rose. "It was the old Gerard again. The food was fabulous, the music was wonderful. The cake sparkled when they brought it in. We talked and joked and danced. Magical.

"And look," she held out her hand. A lovely diamond and ruby ring glistened on her finger. "There's a matching necklace, bracelet and brooch. He gave it to me before we went to bed." Her face suddenly took on a mischievous look. "I hope we didn't disturb you?"

They both laughed.

Gerard appeared at the door.

"Morning," he said. "Wonderful day. Looking forward to breakfast."

He looked affectionately at Rose. "Better leave fairly shortly after breakfast. It's quite a trek back home."

Diana and Art saw them off.

"Thank you for a lovely stay and for all your kindness," said Rose hugging them both.

Gerard shook hands with each of them. "Well done both. My report will go into head office by the end of next week. There's a lot of areas that need smartening up." He looked meaningfully at Diana. "But somehow you've pulled it off. You've obviously got that people touch. Rose is a great judge of character. If she is happy with the service, then you must be doing something right."

Gerard drove off. "Another magical mystery tour for Rose," said Art.

"I think he's worth it," said Diana and they both smiled.

Chapter Ten: The Oasis

"It looks like I'll be going to the Oasis tomorrow night," said Art as he put down the phone.

"The Oasis? Whatever for?" asked Diana.

"Bert says he wants to talk to me. He's got a friend coming and he wants to put him up with us."

"Why doesn't he just book like anyone else? Why drag you to the Oasis?"

"Don't ask me," said Art. "But if it's an opportunity to get him on side, I should take it."

"It all sounds a bit funny to me. He's lives on his own and his house is quite big. Why can't his friend stay there?"

"I've no idea. But I guess we're not going to say 'no' to some possible business. It's been a bit lean of late."

There wasn't an answer to that so Diana didn't make one.

Bert was the village tree warden. He had a somewhat chequered history and was generally regarded as a knowledgeable man but a miserable old bugger. When Art and Diana had bought Ash Meadow he had been particularly vocal in his opinion that they were property developers. He had it on good authority that they intended to make their millions and leave the village with an ugly new housing estate. So he launched a pre-emptive strike. He wrote to the local council objecting to any application for planning permission. When rumour takes a grip it is difficult to shake off. Five years later Minefielders were just beginning to believe Diana and Art wanted to wander round the meadow and not to build on it. This meant they were just eccentrics which was much more acceptable. So the invitation from Bert was a sign that even he felt they were harmless.

It was Bert who owned the Oasis. It could loosely be described as a club. It was based in an underground concrete bunker nestled on the edge of the old airfield and largely hidden from the road. During World War II it had been used for repairing and storing Jeeps and other vehicles. To get there you had to go along an old runway and into a small thicket of trees. There was a tumbledown garage and a mechanic's pit which were now used to store straw. Loads of junk littered the area: old furniture vans, caravans, tyres, bits of engine. It wasn't strictly a men-only club but very few women ever went.

Joe, the local gardener, had invited Art there when they first bought the Old Vicarage and before they had opened the bed and breakfast.

"What's it like?" asked Diana.

"In a word?" said Art. "Horrible! I'm not surprised women don't go there. I shan't be going back."

"Can you be a bit more specific?"

"Well it's underground. You get to it through the remains of a pill box. One of those funny little concrete boxes the government had built during World War II so we could all shoot arrows at Hitler if he happened by. Being underground, it's damp and quite cool. The ceiling is low so it feels claustrophobic. There's a bar of sorts at one end, a few chairs and tables and then a pool table. Very basic."

"Why would anyone go there?"

"The booze is cheap. Everyone knows everyone, so a lot of business deals are done there. And it's out of the way. No doubt there's a lot of after hours drinking."

"However did they get a licence?" asked Diana.

"It's been going a long time. I think they are only licensed for Fridays and Saturdays anyway."

"I'd love to take a look," said Diana.

"I'd leave well alone," said Art. "You might see things that a magistrate shouldn't see!!"

"I wonder why they call it the Oasis? It's a bit of misnomer."

Art had asked the same question. "Joe says it's a haven. A respite from the women folk." He ducked the cushion Diana threw at him.

* * * * * * * * *

Art set off to meet Bert the following evening. He still wasn't back when Diana went to bed at midnight. At 3 am there was a crash on the stairs followed by a lot of giggling.

Diana leapt out of bed and turned on the landing light. Art was still lying on his back at the top of the stairs.

"Hello my love," he slurred. "Sorry, did I wake you?" He waved a hand in front of his face and tried to bring his forefinger to his lips. "Shh... " he said. "Musshant disturb the neighbours." He beamed up at her.

Diana glared.

"Oh dear," Art started to roll over and attempted to get up. "I'm in trouble," he said as he fell flat on his face. He started to giggle. "Don't worry about me," he told the carpet. "I'm perfectly capable."

Diana helped him up and dumped him, none too gently, on the bed in the spare room.

"I love you," burbled Art. "I'm a very lucky man to have a wife like you." And promptly fell asleep.

Diana woke him at 8 am with a mug of coffee. She pulled the curtains back and Art let out a yowl as the sunlight streamed in. He shut his eyes immediately. "You torturer," he complained. "Oh my head." Diana sat down on the end of the bed. Art opened one eye and squinted at her.

"You're enjoying this," he complained.

"Only in proportion to the pain," said Diana drily. "So what happened?"

Art considered for a moment. "I don't remember," he said sheepishly. "It might come back to me in a bit."

"Well come and find me when it does," said Diana and marched out of the room.

"Oh dear," said Art to no one in particular.

* * * * * * * * *

After a shower and another coffee, the pounding started to recede and bits of memory crept back. Art went to find Diana.

"Bert wants to book a friend of his in for next Saturday," he said. "His name is Pete. I've just remembered."

"Is that it?" Diana asked. "You spent eight hours negotiating one night's B&B? How much did you have to drink? You must have spent all the profit."

"We got talking about other stuff and then Captain Adam and Joe arrived. They were followed by Geordie Dave and 'You ain't seen me' Eddie and the time just slipped away. It wasn't as expensive as you think. Beer is only £1 a bottle and the shots are 50p each."

"How does he make a profit?"

"I'm not sure he can do. I think he does it for a hobby as much as anything else."

"So what else did you talk about?"

"I don't really remember but I have a feeling I've agreed to go up there next week when his mate arrives and bring him back here."

Diana gave him that dark look.

"It's a good way of networking. All the locals seem to go up there," Art said fiddling nervously with his shirt buttons.

Diana raised her eyebrows.

"I notice there's some ironing needs doing," Art continued. "I know you hate ironing. Why don't you have a long bath and relax? I'll bring you a drink and then get on with it."

* * * * * * * * * *

Art might have lost his memory but I had watched them all come home. Having poured Eddie into his house, Dave, Joe and Adam had staggered up to the Old Vicarage and had deposited Art on the doorstep. They left each other with expressions of loyalty and brotherhood. All for one and one for all. They looked more like Muscaducks than Musketeers especially when Geordie Dave tried to climb up the beech tree and fell off the first branch.

The Oasis and I have long been old friends despite the very different nature of our work. I've lost count of the number of serious incidents we have averted. For decades, Minefield men have stumbled across the airfield back on to the road and just missed being knocked over by some other late night reveller. The Oasis would let me know they were coming and I would guide their way home by enhancing the light that came from the stars or moon. In return, the Oasis kept me informed of some of the more harebrained schemes that were being plotted inside that concrete bunker.

I had long been aware of Bert's creativity when it came to stocking up at the Oasis. A lot of duty free hooch was dispensed from the optics and even some home brew. It didn't take a genius to work out that this mysterious friend, Pete, was involved, especially when Art announced he would be travelling in a large transit van.

I found my loyalties somewhat conflicted especially as Art seemed to be completely unaware of what was afoot. Bert had been running the gauntlet for many years and, despite a number of raids by police and the customs, had never been caught. There was obviously someone tipping him off. But it was only a matter of time before his luck ran out. And I had a horrible feeling in my mortar that time was fast approaching.

The following weekend all my worst fears were played out.

Bert's friend, Pete, arrived promptly at the Oasis. His transit van was overloaded with a wide range of booze of which Her Majesty had no knowledge. More surprising was the presence and apparent involvement of Captain Adam.

A less likely smuggler would be hard to find. Captain Adam was a nervous man, prone to stress and anxiety attacks, especially where the ladies were concerned. Unfortunately for him, he was regarded as an eligible bachelor. He went to extreme lengths to avoid being invited to dinner parties and being paired up with the latest merry widow. But his attempts to distance himself only made him more attractive and more hotly pursued. Somehow he had been persuaded to use one of the yachts he regularly skippered to carry the illicit cargo. He had brought the bootlegged booze into Southwold from where Pete had collected it. By the time Art, Joe and Geordie Dave arrived it was all safely stashed and the intrepid trio (Bert, Peter and Adam) were enjoying the evening sunshine.

It was turning into quite a session when the phone rang. Bert wandered off to get a better signal. When he reappeared he was white as a sheet.

"Whasup?" called Joe. "You look like you just saw a ghost."

"If only I had," said Bert. "The police are on their way."

"That's OK," called out Art who was already one over the eight. "Let them come and join the party. We could put some music on, have a dance, get the girls up here."

"I got no objections," said Geordie Dave. "Some of my best friends are police officers."

By contrast, Pete and Captain Adam had rapidly sobered up.

"We've got to shift the stuff," shouted Pete. "Quick. Get it back in the van."

"No good," said Bert. "Apparently there's a squad car sitting at the bottom of the road and one on the other side of the airfield. If you can be surrounded by two cars- we're surrounded."

"So what?" said Art. "Bring 'em all over. More the merrier."

Joe was beginning to fit the pieces of the jigsaw together

"How do you know all this Bert?" he asked quietly.

"My contact. Just phoned."

"Well why didn't he phone before?" demanded Captain Adam.

"It was his day off," said Bert defensively.

Geordie Dave started to cotton on. "Is this booze hooky?"

"Of course it is you bloody fool. Now help us to shift it."

"What? Sixty crates of beer and three hundred bottles of whisky, vodka and gin. Oh of course. I'll just stick them up my jumper," shouted Pete

"Ompa, lompa, stick it up your jumper," warbled Art now on his third bottle of cider and away with the fairies.

"I can't afford a police record. I'd never skipper another boat." Captain Adam paced backwards and forwards.

"Sod the police," said Geordie Dave. "If Kate catches me up to anything else dodgy, I'll be in the agricultural business for years to come."

"With two acres," giggled Art. "Don't worry lads. Bulldog spirit. We'll tunnel our way out of the police station. Diana will bury the file in a cake. She's a magistrate you know."

"Tunnels… Tunnels … Hang on a moment. The cogs are turning. Art, you're a genius," yelled Bert.

"How long have we got?" said Joe, ahead of the game as usual.

"Ten minutes, I'd say. They're just waiting for the search warrant."

"Right lads. Follow me. Form an orderly queue. Bert you'll have to stall them."

Joe ran back into the Oasis and leapt behind the bar. He shifted some shelves to reveal an old wooden door. The door opened on to a tunnel connecting the concrete bunker and the airfield. It had been dug out as part of a training exercise and was used by US pilots and crew to reach the planes without being shelled. Bert had found it again decades later when he started up the bar.

"I haven't used that tunnel for years," Bert called after them. "If it hasn't fallen in, you'll come out near the removal lorry. Stash the booze in there for the time being."

The next ten minutes were frantic as Joe, Captain Adam, Pete and Geordie Dave passed the booze in a chain down the tunnel. Art went to help but tripped over the stairs and knocked himself out. They hauled him into a chair, threw a jug of water over him and left him singing his medley of songs by the Beatles.

Bert's informant was right on with the timing. Ten minutes later flashing lights were seen on the runway heading straight towards them. Two police cars screeched to a halt and Sergeant Boxer got out.

"Evening Bert," he said.

"Hello Sergeant Boxer," said Bert. "It's a while since we last saw you. You should have called. I'm running a bit low on pork scratchings."

"I'll get by with a little help from my friends." Art's voice drifted up from the Bunker.

"Who's that?"

"Oh it's just Art Selby from the Old Vicarage B&B. His wife Diana's a magistrate you know."

"I am a spaceman," sang Art. "I am a spaceman and you are a walrus. Co Co Cochu."

"I have a warrant to search these premises," said Sergeant Boxer. "We are looking for contraband."

"Never heard of them," said Bert. "Do they sing any blues?"

Sergeant Boxer ignored him. "This is Mr Light from Her Majesty's Revenue and Customs. We have reason to believe you have been selling alcohol on which duty hasn't been paid."

"Sergeant Pepper's lonely hearts club band ..." Art offered from below.

"Can't you shut him up?" asked Sergeant Boxer. "He'd give an aspirin a headache."

"Let me see that warrant for a minute?" Bert made great show of reading the warrant.

"Quit stalling Bert," said Sergeant Boxer. "It's not as if you haven't seen one before."

"Yes," said Bert. "And that's my point. This is the third time. It amounts to harassment. That's what it is and I've a good mind to complain."

"Take it up with my superiors." Sergeant Boxer had lost patience and pushed past Bert.

"We hope that you enjoy the show..." Art serenaded as he walked down the stairs.

Three police officers and Mr Light followed.

Just as they disappeared downstairs and, in the spirit of a well rehearsed farce, Dave popped up like a jack-in-the-box from the mechanic's pit. He saw Art and gave the thumbs up.

"I get by with a little help from my friends," Art sang and promptly collapsed again.

The original knock on the head had taken its toll and Art became unrousable. More blue lights were called and Art was stretchered off to hospital. The search was further scuppered when Sergeant Boxer and the other police officers were summoned to attend a 999 call involving poachers and guns on the Bramingfield estate.

"Don't think I won't be back," said Sergeant Boxer.

"Be careful out there," responded Bert. "The Bramingfield Bunnies need your protection."

It was Pete who had dialled 999.

"A real masterstroke," chuckled Bert as the gang came trooping into the bunker. They had waved Art off in the ambulance and called Diana.

"Did you get it all out?"

"Every last drop," said Joe.

"Well that calls for a celebration." Bert cracked open a bottle of whisky. "To Sergeant Boxer. May all his problems be small, pink and with curly tails."

He turned to Captain Adam.

"So when's the next shipment coming in, my old mate?"

"You've got to be kidding," said Adam. "I've aged twenty years this evening. Never again."

"You can count me out too," said Geordie Dave. "How old are we? I stopped doing this kind of caper thirty years ago. I'm a pipe and slippers man these days."

Bert looked at the sea of faces. "OK, OK I get the message. Back to the cash and carry."

"I'll drink to that," said Joe and raised his glass.

Chapter Eleven: Animal Instincts

"Are we going to regret this?" Diana asked Art. "Mum and two daughters. One a fifteen year old. All in one room. You can't get much more cramped than that. Why don't they just stay with their grandparents?"

"It's only for two nights," said Art. "Perhaps our room is bigger than theirs. Perhaps grandparents are too fragile to be descended on full time. Come on. How bad can it be?"

Diana winced. She had three sisters and she well remembered the bitter sibling rivalries and arguments that escalated into full scale fights. Memories that, even now, coloured their ongoing relationships.

"They lost their father last year?" she asked.

"Yes. It was all very sudden. A heart attack. Totally unexpected. Mum says they are all still adjusting."

"Poor things, said Diana. "I think I'll bake a cake."

Art was amused. "That's your answer to everything isn't it? Someone's lost a dog, a leg, a father. A homemade cake will put it right."

"Well it never hurts and sometimes it shows you care. I didn't say it was a silver bullet."

The doorbell rang. Sacha (mum), Kylie (aged eight and a half) and Suzanne (aged fifteen) had arrived.

"Welcome to the Old Vicarage," Art beamed at them.

"It doesn't look very old," said Suzanne.

"No. It's old as in 'ex' or 'formerly known as'," explained Art.

"That's ridiculous," said Suzanne.

"So we are beginning to realise," said Art.

Suzanne's sulky manner and constant scowling was not helped by her appearance. She was overweight, covered in acne, had shaved half her head and dyed the other half green. There was a ruby red stud in her lip.

Sacha stepped forward. "We're delighted to be here aren't we girls?" Suzanne and Kylie looked anything but delighted. "It's really good of you to put us all up. I hope it hasn't put you out too much."

"Of course not," said Diana coming out of the kitchen. "Come on in. Art can show you the room and I'll make you a cup of tea."

"I don't drink tea," said Kylie.

"How does hot chocolate sound?"

"With cream and a flake?" asked Kylie.

"Kylie! Don't be so ungracious." Sacha was clearly embarrassed.

Diana laughed. "I can't do cream and flakes but if I put out some marshmallow pieces, chocolate chips and hundreds and thousands, do you think you could make something yourself?"

"Could I ever!" said Kylie and smiled. She caught sight of Mr Mistoffelees. "Is that your cat?" she asked.

"Yes," said Art. "Meet Mr Mistoffelees otherwise known as MM." MM sauntered over and did her usual meerkat impression which involved squatting on hind legs and raising her front paws in the air. It was a party trick that never failed to impress and usually involved treats.

Kylie was smitten. "That's so cool," she said scratching MM's head. "I want a cat but I can't have one because Suzanne is allergic to them."

The bantam chickens, Faith, Hope and Charity, sauntered around the corner, wobbling from side to side. As usual when they saw Art they came scampering over. Everybody, even Suzanne, had to laugh at their antics.

Suzanne refused a drink and went straight to the bedroom, headphones clamped firmly to her head. "She's in a punk phase," said Sacha.

"Isn't she thirty years too late?" asked Art.

"Oh there are still dedicated followers. Earlier this year it was Goths. She was dressed as a vampire for weeks. I'm not sure which is worse."

Mum Sacha seemed completely worn out. Her complexion was pale and there were deep purple rings beneath her eyes. She looked like a Goth herself.

"We haven't been up to see my mum and dad since Chris, my husband, passed away. There is room in their house but they are both quite elderly and Dad has just had his hip replaced. With things the way they are …. The girls can be a bit difficult," she confided as if we hadn't noticed. "We thought it better if we had our own space."

* * * * * * * * * *

"It's going to take more than homemade cake to sort that family out," said Art later. "Sacha has lost control. Did you hear the way those girls spoke to her. Even Kylie can clearly be a little madam. Sacha seems to be constantly criticising her kids or apologising for them. There's no respect there at all."

The bickering they had witnessed was an amuse bouche to what came later. Diana and Art were watching TV when they heard an awful din coming from the B&B room.

"Give that to me ..."

"I hate you ...."

"You stupid little idiot, that's mine."

"Suzanne stop that immediately ... give Kylie back her iPod."

"I hate you. You're a useless bitch. I wish you had died and not Dad."

There was a crash as something was hurled across the room and then the sound of crying.

It's not easy to be the objective narrator when the family you are describing is falling apart at the seams. My heart went out to this embittered and broken trio but the anger was too raw and recent for any of us to bring about change. We all had to hope the raging storm would wear itself out.

The next morning battle recommenced at breakfast. Kylie opened every tablet of jam and marmalade and made a mud pie. Meantime Suzanne idly flicked spoonfuls of cornflakes and milk across the table. Both ignored Sacha's feeble and unconvincing protests.

It was only after they had left to visit the grandparents and Diana was cleaning their room that she discovered the broken mirror, the ripped duvet and the huge stain in the carpet. She showed them to Art.

"What are we going to do? Do you think Sacha was planning to own up or apologise? We're a business, not a crèche. The cost of putting this lot right will be more than we make. Sacha just seems to have given up. She threatens consequences but doesn't see them through. There are no boundaries. No wonder she didn't want to inflict them full time on the grandparents. Oh lucky us! We got the family from hell instead. I can't let this pass. I'll have a word when she gets back."

Diana was out when the family returned earlier than anticipated. Kylie had been caught stealing money from her grandmother's purse. The drama escalated into a crisis and a full scale row ensued that drew in everyone. It only ended when Suzanne stormed off having publicly and loudly called her mother a 'shabby f**king whore'.

Art found Sacha swinging backwards and forwards on the swing seat, tears pouring down her cheeks.

"I'm sorry," Sacha said through tears. "It's just I'm at the end of my tether. I'm a special needs teacher for heaven's sake. I'm supposed to be able to deal with challenging behaviour. But all the rule books go out of the window when it's your own family. There are times when I hate Chris for leaving me with this. But more and more I find myself hating the girls and just wishing them out of my life."

"You don't mean that," said Art.

"May be, may be not. But I seem to have lost me in all this. What about how I feel? I hate the person I have become and I hate the girls for making me this way."

"You really don't mean that. Don't even say it. You have no idea how lucky you are to have those girls. Giving up on them is the last thing you should be doing. You need to get a grip."

Art got up and walked away leaving Sacha stunned and angry by turns.

Diana arrived back from the shops shortly after. She saw Sacha in the garden and walked over to have a chat about the morning's disruption. She didn't get very far.

"I think I've upset your husband," stated Sacha coldly. "He's just been very rude."

"That's not like Art." Diana held back a desire to leap to his defence. "What did he say?"

"It wasn't so much 'what' as how he said it," said Sacha. "He told me to get a grip."

"Why would he say such a thing?" asked Diana.

"We had an incident at mum's. I was just telling him how I felt about the girls, how they wind me up and I can't control them."

"Did you say anything else?"

"I may have said something about wishing they were out of my life, but I didn't mean it," said Sacha.

"Ah …" said Diana.

"What do you mean … 'Ah' …?"

"You've probably noticed that Art and I haven't any children. But Art did have a family before we met. A long time ago. His previous partner had two children both from different partners and she was pregnant with one by him. By all accounts he was a doting stepdad. But she had bi polar disorder and during one particularly manic episode she left him. In fact she went much further and actively prevented him from seeing the children. She made allegations of child abuse which were unsubstantiated but helped her get a temporary restraining order so he couldn't see any of the children. It's hard for dads now but thirty five years ago an unmarried, unofficial stepfather had no rights. He couldn't get anyone to see just how vulnerable she was until it was too late."

"Too late?" asked Sacha.

"To cut a long and miserable story short. During one of her depressive episodes, she suffocated both children and then took her own life."

"Oh goodness. How terrible."

"Yes. It's a pretty gruesome story and he doesn't usually talk about it. But he has never really believed he couldn't have done something to prevent the tragedy. So, whether you meant it or not, when you said you wanted the children out of your life…"

"It brought it all back …" finished Sacha.

"Art will know he's put two and two together and made five. He shouldn't have done it. But I thought you should hear the story at least - just to explain."

"He's right about one thing though," said Sacha.

"What's that?" asked Diana.

"I should take a grip. My own flesh and blood for goodness' sake."

"Do you think "taking a grip" might sometimes mean asking for help?" suggested Diana.

Sacha smiled grimly. "Stop pretending it's alright, when it isn't?"

"Something like that," said Diana.

Sacha got up. "I should go and find Kylie."

"She's over by the trees with Art. It looks like MM is playing to an audience again. You should go and join them."

"I think I will," said Sacha. She walked towards them both. Kylie saw her coming and raced across the lawn. "Mummy come and see MM. He's hugging trees. He's so funny. I wish we had a cat like him."

"How would you like to sleep in MM's room tonight?" asked Art.

Kylie's eyes widened. "How?"

"MM sleeps in one of our upstairs bedrooms. If you ask your mum very nicely, she might let you stay in that room tonight. If you were very lucky MM would snuggle up with you."

Kylie turned to Sacha. "Please .. pretty please with sugar and spices."

"What about Granny's money and this morning's escapade?" asked Sacha. "You don't get treats for doing bad things."

Kylie thought for a moment. "I'll go round and say sorry. I'll give her back the chocolates she bought me and clean gramp's car."

"That sounds a very adult thing to do," said Sacha. "OK. If you show me you can behave responsibly, you can sleep with MM tonight."

Art winked at Sacha. "Nice one," he said. "One down, one to go."

"Any ideas?" asked Sacha.

"Nope," said Art and they both laughed. "But a problem shared is half way to a problem solved, don't you think?"

* * * * * * * * * *

Suzanne meantime had stomped off but having nowhere to go found herself back at the Old Vicarage. Rather than come into the house, she turned into the allotments and wandered past the different plots until she found the chicken co-operative. She didn't hear Joe, one of our chicken co-operative founders, until he was at her shoulder.

"Arternoon," he said. "I see you're admiring our chickens."

"No I'm not," said Suzanne. "Why would I be interested in those flea bitten stupid critters?"

"They're far from stupid," said Joe. "Each one is an individual. You see that brown Orpington over there?" He pointed to a beautiful red-brown bird. "Her name's Suzanne. Just like yours. She was a right scrappy mangy creature when she got here. Not surprising given she'd spent all her life as a battery hen. And now look at her."

"How do you know my name is Suzanne?"

"Bit difficult not to know it when you and your sister are screeching like barn owls at each other all the time. You don't half give your poor mum the run-around."

"What's it to you?" asked Suzanne defensively.

"Nothing except the noise you make puts the birds off laying. As I get the eggs today, I don't take kindly to you lot squawking louder than they do."

Suzanne laughed in spite of herself.

"Do you want to help feed them?" asked Joe.

"Me? Chickens? Won't they peck me?"

"You're a townie and no mistake. What's up scaredy-cat? Do you think with your green quiff they might mistake you for a cockerel?"

Suzanne hesitated.

"Come on. Contrary to popular belief they don't bite."

Joe showed Suzanne how to handle, feed and clean the birds and their coop. The birds arched their backs and flattened their wings so she could stroke them.

"You're a natural," said Joe. "I've never seen birds take so well to a stranger. See if you can find some eggs."

Art, Sacha and Kylie came across about twenty minutes later. Suzanne was squatting on the grass with a chicken in her arms and nine eggs in a basket at her feet.

"Joe's going to help me design an enclosure so that we can keep chickens at home," she announced. "We've got the room haven't we?"

Sacha looked dubious. "Don't they take a lot of looking after?"

"Of course not, stupid. I can do it before and after school."

Joe coughed pointedly.

"Sorry. I didn't mean to call you stupid. But, honestly, they don't need a great deal of time. Tell her Joe."

"You could start off with a couple of the bantams, like Art and Diana have. See how you get on and build from there," said Joe.

"What about it mum?" said Suzanne.

Sacha thought for a moment. "Well …" she began.

"Brilliant," said Suzanne. "When mum says '*well*' like that she always means '*yes*'."

"If Suzanne's having chickens, can I have a cat?" asked Kylie.

"Steady on," laughed Sacha. "One step at a time. That's a much bigger deal especially with Suzanne's allergy."

"Are you allergic to cat hair?" asked Joe?

"Ever since I was little," said Suzanne.

"You can grow out of these things. Chickens and cats are different but it's usually an allergy to the dust and dust mites. When did you last notice it?"

"I don't go near cats so I don't know."

"Might be worth checking again. You don't seem to have been affected by MM. Even if you are allergic there are some cat breeds that moult less. Where there's a will, there's a way. But there needs to be a will …" He looked seriously at Suzanne.

"If we check out my allergy levels, will you help me with the chicken coop?" asked Suzanne.

"It's not a bargain," said Joe. "I'll help you because it's a good thing to do."

"Then let's get my allergy levels checked anyway." Suzanne looked directly at Sacha. "Because it's a good thing to do."

The group watched Suzanne put the chickens back in the coop.

"OK troops," said Sacha. "Kylie has Gramp's car to wash. And then we need to find somewhere for tea. What do you fancy?"

"Fish and chips," said Kylie.

"Pizza," from Suzanne.

"Fish and chips."

"What about somewhere that sells both?" suggested Sacha.

"Suits me," said Suzanne.

"And me," added Kylie.

The girls walked back to the Old Vicarage and Sacha turned to Joe.

"Thank you," she said. "You may just have saved my sanity."

Joe looked slightly embarrassed and scratched his chin. It sounded like sandpaper. He rubbed his gnarled, work-worn hands together. "Anyone who loves animals gets my vote. She's just needs some time and a purpose. It'll work out. I'll come over tomorrow at 10 o'clock to help her sketch out some designs for a chicken coop. I hope that's OK?"

"Of course," said Sacha. "Thank you again."

Joe picked up the eggs. "I'll be seeing you then," he said. "Arternoon."

"What a nice man," said Sacha looking after him. "How old is he? He looks eighty but he moves like a much younger man. You'd never guess he had a heart of gold. Just shows you can't judge a book by its cover."

"Ain't that the truth," said Art.

Chapter 12: Ghost Busters

Diana and Art watched in dismay and shock as the ambulance staff wheeled out the body of Mr Jones, followed by the weeping, newly widowed, Mrs Jones.

"He was an elderly gentleman who died peacefully in his sleep," Dr Scribe tried to reassure them. "No one could have known and there was nothing that could have been done."

"Thank you Doctor. At least that's something." Art was on automatic pilot.

"Does Mrs Jones have any relatives or friends that need to be informed?"

"Yes, we've called her daughter and son-in-law. They are on their way," said Diana.

After everyone had left, Diana and Art made coffee and sat outside on the patio, rocking gently backwards and forwards on the swing seat.

"It's not working is it?" Art said. "The B&B. Perhaps we ought to shut it down. Would you want to sleep in a bed someone had just died in?"

"We could change the bed," said Diana.

"There's still the room. Would you want to sleep in a room where someone had died?"

"They don't have to know."

"Don't kid yourself," said Art. "Mr and Mrs Jones were friends of Daisy. You might as well broadcast it on News at Ten."

"It won't put everyone off."

"How would you feel? I don't think I'd want to sleep in a room where someone has just died."

"We could redecorate. Give it a complete facelift."

"Let's face it. We're making hardly any money. We have a low occupancy rate. The business barely has a pulse. It's a real tie. You certainly can't retire on it. And now it looks like it will cost more than it will bring in. I think this episode is a death blow for more than just Mr Jones."

It was all true. Diana didn't have an answer and I couldn't deny the logic either. But all of us felt we were losing more than a business. I knew, more than anyone else, the difference we had made to so many of the people who had stayed here: even if it was just some peace and time to think. Diana and Art didn't expect to make a big profit but it didn't make sense to run a business that was losing money. I think we all felt we were at a crossroads.

"Joe's friend, Mr Scragg, is coming next weekend," said Diana. "Do you think I better ring and tell him what's happened? He may not want to stay here now."

"It's only fair," agreed Art.

* * * * * * * * *

"So you see," said Diana. "We fully understand if you'd rather not come."

"Nonsense," a Welsh voice boomed down the phone. "We've all got to go at some point, haven't we?

"Anyway depending on who the deceased was and how he died, there might be some additional psychic phenomena to measure. You say he was an old man? That he died peacefully in his sleep? No suggestion of foul play?"

"No. Absolutely not." Diana tried to reassure him.

"That's a pity. No chance it was suicide?"

"Nobody seems to think so."

"Well never mind. If there is some unresolved business he may still be around. We'll just have to see, won't we? So absolutely no problem and see you next weekend. I'm really looking forward to it."

"That's good Mr Scragg."

"Call me Darren."

Diana hesitated. "Would I be right in thinking that you are a sort of ghost buster, Darren?"

Darren Scragg chuckled. "That's one word for it. I like to think I take a more scientific approach and I'm afraid it's much less exciting. Not a lot of running around with zappers."

"You do realise that when we say 'old' vicarage, we actually mean 'formerly known as' a vicarage. It's not an old building," said Diana.

"My dear young lady. Firstly you have had two deaths in the house to my knowledge. Secondly you are on the edge of a World War II airfield from which many people lost their lives, not least from the ammunition dump explosion. Thirdly, Minefield was inhabited at least as far back as Anglo Saxon and Norman times if the Domesday book is to be believed.

Who knows but there may have been settlement on the site you now occupy. Who knows what secrets are buried in the land, or voices that still echo in the night air. My excitement and anticipation increases just thinking about it. You mustn't worry about a thing. I will see you next week." The phone went dead.

Diana relayed all this to Art.

"What's the second death?"

"I think he must be referring to the child of one of the vicars. Paul Sharp. They lost one of their children in a car accident when they were in Minefield," said Diana.

"So the only market we can rely on are eccentrics with a morbid interest in death. That feels like a very a select group. I think it answers the question of whether we can keep going. We'll make Mr Scragg our last customer."

* * * * * * * * *

Darren Scragg arrived promptly at 3 pm the following Saturday and Joe came across to introduce him.

"Arternoon," he said. "This is Darren. He's here to check out whether there is any truth in recent reports of psychic phenomena in Minefield. I've agreed to lend a hand in exchange for some help on the allotments. We're collecting produce for the old folks. Sunday is the harvest festival lunch."

"What reports of psychic phenomena?" asked Art. "That's the first I've heard of it."

"There's a whole host of ghosts out there. Virtually everyone's seen them at some time," said Joe.

"Who's everyone?" pursued Art.

"Well Geordie Dave saw someone on the airfield last Christmas."

"If he was on his way back from the Oasis, he was probably nine parts to the wind," said Art. "Go on."

"Then there's Daisy. She saw a pilot in his US air force flying jacket walking down the high street. That was early in the morning just as she was getting into her car."

"Was that the time she drove into the telephone box on the other side of the road to avoid hitting a child? The 'child' being a 'men at work' road sign?"

"I've heard something myself round near the back of the church," Joe continued undaunted.

"And that could have been anything: pheasant, rabbits, fox. It might even have been that wretched homing mole coming up for air."

"Well you can't gainsay Mildred. She's straight as a die and she's both seen and heard stuff on this road. Sound of planes, firing, voices, flashing lights."

Art found that one a bit more difficult to dismiss. Mildred at ninety six was as sharp as a button. Thrice a Times Crossword champion finalist and former head teacher of the village school. She brooked no nonsense from anyone. Art couldn't imagine she would entertain any frivolous notions of the supernatural.

Darren broke in. "Now, now boys. No need to start an argument. I'm merely here to check if there's anything in the gossip. I'll be taking the equipment up on to the airfield tonight and we'll walk the land. What time does it get dark?"

"Mid September – certainly by 8.30 pm," said Art.

"Right Joe. Come and collect me at 8 pm," said Darren putting an end to any further squabbling.

* * * * * * * * *

That was the last we saw of Darren until the next day. In spite of his cynicism Art was very curious to hear what had happened. So he hovered near the doorway when Diana asked.

"Nothing conclusive, I'm afraid," said Darren. "Not yet anyway. There are some minor blips on the radar but they could be anything. We're going to come close to the village tonight. Starting with the road junction at the bottom of your field."

"What time did you get in?" asked Diana.

"Oh about 3 am."

"If you're going to help Joe on the allotment, you'll be out for the count."

"Rubbish. A few late nights never hurt anyone," laughed Darren.

During the course of the day we saw Darren helping Joe gather offerings from the allotment owners and box them up. The harvest lunch was the idea of our newest Vicar, Sarah Long. She was uncharitably called the eco-warrior because of her passion for environmental causes. Her current crusade was around carbon footprints. On the face of it a locally produced and communally prepared meal to celebrate bringing in the harvest seemed a great idea. And it had really caught on with enthusiastic allotment owners keen to make a contribution. Even Joe had been up for it.

"I don't hold any truck with religion, Vicar," he had said bluntly as they chatted over the allotment gates opposite the Old Vicarage. "But I'd be glad to support the old folks. We'll donate the eggs from the co-operative and I'll box up produce from the other allotment owners and bring it across."

Sarah Long smiled inwardly as Joe talked about helping the old folk. No one knew how old he was but it was somewhere between sixty and one hundred.

After a long day digging and packing Joe and Darren delivered the produce to the village hall ready to be cooked the following day. Diana had been roped into food preparation following her great success with the scones at the village gardens' open day.

"Will you be joining us for lunch tomorrow?" she asked Darren as he came in to wash up and prepare for the night's vigil.

"Wouldn't miss it," he said. "It'll be a lovely end to the weekend."

"He's a nice old boy," commented Art later. "Pity he's wasting so much time on this psychic rubbish."

"Everyone needs a hobby," said Diana. "Look at you with your old radios, communing with people living thousands of miles away that don't speak English and you can barely hear. Some people might call that a waste of time."

"Which just shows what you know about ham radio amateurs," said Art hotly.

"I rest my case," said Diana.

* * * * * * * * *

Joe came round at 8 pm and he and Darren set off again.

"Did you see the hip flask?" laughed Art. "I expect they'll see quite a lot of the spirit world tonight. It's certainly getting chilly."

The next morning a very buoyant Darren sat down to breakfast.

"There was definitely something," he said. "We got some really strong readings which came and went."

"Where did you go?" asked Diana.

"We were up on the slopes before the airfield. The maps show there used to be a clay pit in that area."

"That's where the house was bombed," said Diana. "The rubble from its remains was used to cover up the unexploded bomb at the bottom of our field."

She could see Darren was trying to contain his excitement. "Well it's early days. We need to visit the site on other nights and I think I should interview this Mildred. She sounds very level headed. And I'll do some digging in the records. We may be on to something."

He turned to Diana. "Could I stay another night? I'd like to take some more readings."

"Of course," she said. "On condition you tell me what you think you've uncovered?"

"It really is too early to say with any degree of certainty," said Darren. "But the increased energy suggests something traumatic. Something trapped in the landscape that keeps replaying. We might only see parts of it under certain atmospheric conditions.

"I have seen similar energy surges," he continued. "Usually you can trace it to events in the recent past and there's often some connection with unfinished business."

"Like if someone was murdered?" asked Diana. "And the killer wasn't caught. Or committed suicide and was buried in ground that wasn't consecrated? They used to put a stake in the heart of self killers and bury the body at a crossroads just to add to the confusion. Come to think of it, there's a crossroads just down from where you are working at the moment. Is this the sort of unfinished business you mean?"

Darren was a bit hesitant. "Well I suppose so but those examples are a bit extreme. Unfinished business doesn't have to be quite that dramatic. It's just a story not yet told."

"So the quest is to find the story and to tell it? And does that make a difference?"

"In my experience, it seems to quieten things down. Of course there may be more than one story. And just understanding the story may not resolve it. Anyway we shouldn't get ahead of ourselves. It may be nothing or there may be some perfectly natural explanation for increased energy levels. Electricity, magnetism, radio waves could all have an impact."

"But you think there is something don't you?" Diana persisted.

"Let's say I'm cautiously optimistic," said Darren. "We'll know more tomorrow."

He got up. "In the meantime we've both got a harvest meal to get ready."

* * * * * * * * * *

There were plenty of volunteers at the village hall to help prepare the lunch. There was to be a stew based on the allotment vegetables, with jacket potatoes and locally supplied beef. Dessert was blackberry and apple with the apples taken from the allotment orchard and the blackberries freshly picked from hedgerows. Apple juice and raspberry cordial were the beverages of the day. Everything had been grown within a five mile radius. The Rev Sarah Long was co-ordinating proceedings and set Diana to peeling apples and scrubbing potatoes while Darren prepared the vegetables for the stew.

There were about twenty five guests in total. At 1 pm the Rev Sarah said grace and everyone sat down to eat.

Art, as usual, had ducked out. He was busy tinkering with his latest old radio when the phone rang. It was Diana.

"Art," she said and sounded quite stressed. "Can you round some people up and come and help. Something's gone very wrong."

"What's up?"

"People are acting very strangely and I'm worried there may be an accident."

"Go on."

"Well there's lots of giggling."

"That's good isn't it?" said Art who didn't want to interrupt his afternoon's leisure.

"Yes but they are laughing at everything and nothing. Mrs Jones and Mr Handle have turned up the music and are trying to dance the Charleston. With his back and her dodgy knees, I'm worried there may be an accident. And Tom and Eric have just gone outside. Tom is climbing the bottle bank and Eric is trying to walk on the church wall. They're both eighty if they're a day."

"Where's Rev Long?"

"Well that's even more surreal. She and half the group are congo-ing around the car park singing '*We plough the fields and scatter*'."

"I'm on my way," said Art. Then as an afterthought. "Have you eaten or drunk anything yourself?"

"Only the apple juice. I was a bit queasy this morning so I didn't feel like eating."

"Stay put. Just try and discourage any extreme sports. No swinging from the bell tower or sky diving from the village hall roof."

Art phoned Joe and Geordie Dave and within ten minutes they were at the village hall. The exuberant chaos was beginning to subside. Tom had been coaxed off the bottle bank and was lying slumped against the stage complaining of a headache and swirling bright colours.

"Water," called Art. "Keep them hydrated. I'm calling an ambulance."

* * * * * * * * * *

Two hours later, Joe, Darren, Diana and Art walked in to the lounge, back at the Old Vicarage, and collapsed on the settees.

"How are you feeling Darren?" asked Diana.

"A bit funny but getting there," said Darren shaking his head. "I'm just so sorry," he said for the thirtieth time.

"You weren't to know they were magic mushrooms," said Diana soothingly.

"Fifteen people taken to hospital," groaned Joe.

"Yes but everyone will make a full recovery. It's just a precaution because of their age," said Diana.

"Look on the bright side," said Art. "Some of them haven't had so much fun for years."

"I just thought it would be nice to have mushrooms in the stew," said Darren.

"Where did you find them?" asked Joe.

"They were in the allotment at the bottom of the orchard."

"You're lucky the police weren't called," said Joe. "Poor Reverend Long will never live this down. Thanks to you she might just have presided over the mass murder of half of her parishioners."

Darren looked crestfallen. "Does this mean you won't be coming with me tonight?"

"Are you kidding? I'm not letting you out of my sight from now on. Goodness knows what new destruction you will wreak."

"Are you really fit to go?" asked Diana.

"I'm sure I will be with a few hours' sleep," said Darren. "Big piece of investigation tonight," he said cheering up.

"Well, I'll make a flask of chocolate and bring it down to you around midnight, just to make sure," said Diana.

"That was very good of you," remarked Art later on.

"What was?" said Diana burying her head in the paper.

"Making a flask of hot chocolate. At midnight."

"Hm. Oh that – it's the least I could do."

What's going on?" said Art. "What are you up to?"

"Nothing."

"Yes you are," said Art. "They've drawn you into their harebrained scheme. You're going ghost hunting!"

"I just thought I'd pop down and see what they are doing," said Diana flicking through the pages. "Aren't you curious, especially in the light of the energy surge Darren has picked up?"

"You don't really believe there are supernatural beings out there?"

"I'm open minded but I'm certainly interested in the process."

"Well," said Art. "I might come with you. I don't want you wandering around in the dark. But it will be a waste of time."

Diana grinned and turned another page.

* * * * * * * * *

At midnight, Diana and Art left to join the others. As they were just down the road, opposite the bottom of Ash Meadow,

I was able to observe directly what happened. The one advantage you humans have over us is your legs. But this time I got to see for myself.

Joe and Darren were sitting on fishing stools in the middle of a grassy slope. The slope led to the World War II airfield and runways. It had been laid to grass for a number of years now and was used by Minefielders to walk their dogs. All signs of the bombed house were obliterated but there were a number of Ordnance Survey maps dating back over 150 years so we knew where it had stood.

Darren was wearing headphones and watching the movement of electronic impulses on a sort of oscilloscope. Joe was holding what looked like a Geiger counter which periodically crackled as it passed information down the line and into the oscilloscope.

"How's it going?" said Diana, producing plastic mugs and opening the flask of hot chocolate.

"Nothing much, so far. It seems much quieter than last night. There's a couple of deckchairs if you want to take a pew."

It was chilly but not freezing and there was a clear night sky. Minefield had no street lamps to spoil the view. Diana spotted the Plough, the Seven Sisters and Orion's belt but that was her limit. Her tablet had an application that plotted the constellations and, after 10 minutes of watching Darren fiddle with his oscilloscope, she wished she'd bought it. An early childhood spent fishing with her father had taught her how boring men's hobbies could be.

After about half an hour they heard the distant rumble of thunder.

Minefield was part of a community of villages and market towns that had developed around the River Waveney. The river ran along the Norfolk/Suffolk border and into the sea at Lowestoft. It was the southern tip of what were known as the Norfolk Broads, a set of man made navigable waters popular with holiday makers. Thunder often rumbled around the valley for half an hour with no sign of rain so they decided to stay put. It was usually accompanied by the most spectacular sheet lightning making a terrific light show. Tonight was no exception.

"I imagine this will increase activity on your Geiger counter," remarked Art as another lightning flash opened up the sky.

"Yes," admitted Darren. "There'll be no reliable readings now. We might as well call it a night and enjoy the show."

The group lapsed into silence, awed by the power enveloping them.

Diana was the first to speak.

"That's a strange noise," she said. "It's been going on for a few seconds but it doesn't sound like thunder. It's got a lower pitch, more of a rumbling sound. Surely there aren't any combine harvesters around at this time of year?"

They all listened. The noise persisted.

"It sounds more like a plane than an agricultural vehicle," said Art. "And it's coming closer."

The rumble got louder and louder until it seemed to be overhead. It was almost deafening. At the same time, they heard repeating gunfire, the wailing of sirens and saw large circles of light in the sky.

"It's coming straight at us," shouted Joe.

Instinctively they all dived to the ground, covering their ears from the noise which was now insupportable. We all (me included) heard an explosion followed by screaming voices, more gunfire and then a crash. It was all over in 10 seconds.

Darren was the first to raise his head. "Is everyone OK?"

Art got up and looked round. "It must have been a helicopter. The airforce is always doing late night low flying manoeuvres. We need to get help. Can anyone see where it crashed?"

They all looked round.

"There's nothing here," said Joe.

The thunder rumbled in the distance and there was another flash of light.

Diana picked up the deckchair which had been knocked over as they dived to the ground. She sat down. "Did we all just experience the same thing? A plane, ground fire, a crash, adults and children screaming."

"We can't have," said Art.

"So what was it?" asked Joe

"Is it possible the past has just been replayed in the present?" asked Diana.

"I think that's exactly what has happened," said Darren.

"Even if it's true, no one will believe us. I don't believe us and I saw it!" said Joe.

"And don't forget it all comes at the end of the day when half the village has been drugged by a magic mushroom stew," said Art.

"That's an unfortunate sequence of events," agreed Darren.

"Who cares what other people think? We all saw and heard the same thing. We know!" said Diana.

"But what does it all mean?" asked Art. "Why here?"

"There must be some unfinished business? Some untold story?" mused Diana. She started to shiver.

"We've all had a shock," said Darren. "What say we call it a night and talk about it tomorrow? It looks like I'll be staying here a few more days. We've got a lot of leads here. There are people in the village who still have a memory of that time and I need to do some research. I'll look for some records of the cottage that was bombed. I'm sure that holds the key."

"I'll take you to see Mildred, tomorrow," said Joe. "She was around then as a land army girl. She'll probably remember."

"Why not invite her to ours in the evening?" said Art. "Diana has to work tomorrow and it would be good for us all to hear what she has to say."

"Agreed," said Darren. "I'll spend the day digging. I've got quite a few contacts now from previous research, so it shouldn't take long to track down some records."

* * * * * * * * * *

The next evening at 7 pm Darren, Diana, Art and Joe sat down in the lounge with Mildred.

"So," she said with a knowing smile. "You've heard the planes."

"Yes we had an amazing display of light, noise, gunfire and voices, including children, last night. It was during the thunderstorm," said Diana.

"You've had the works," said Mildred.

"How often have you experienced it?" asked Darren.

"Oh several times. But many years ago. It was usually late in the evening, sometimes the early hours of the morning after I'd finished marking. I'd go for a bike ride round the aerodromes. When I came past your way I would hear the rumble of distant planes. Because it was often a hot night I was never entirely sure whether I'd heard the rumble of thunder or something else. Then one night, about thirty years ago, I got the full works: the gunfire, the cries, the explosion. I've never forgotten it. I still have nightmares even now. I wake up shaking and sweating. That poor family."

"What family?" everyone asked together.

Mildred looked surprised. "Why the Davies," she said. "I thought you knew."

Darren spoke up. "I found something today in an old police report. It basically states that in April 1944 the local police attended following a bombing by a German Dornier. The report says that a house was destroyed and all occupants, Mr and Mrs Davies and their children died on impact. It also talks about a second unexploded bomb which must be the one that landed at the bottom of your meadow. I suppose it's a reflection of the times that the documents focus more on the unexploded bomb. The Dornier crashed after being shot down. The crew were all killed."

"I guess there was nothing the authorities could do to help the dead so they concentrated on avoiding more fatalities," said Art.

"I was just a nipper then," said Joe. "But I do remember something of all this. There was great excitement amongst us boys about the German plane and the unexploded bomb. I didn't really know the Davies though. They were incomers."

"The voices we heard must have been the Davies," said Diana.

"Mr and Mrs Davies had three children. Tom was seven, Lizzy was four and then there was Tina, who was two," said Mildred. "I remember Lizzy particularly. She was a pretty little girl, very wilful, into everything."

"The reports I've seen suggest that only four bodies were recovered: two adults, a boy and a girl," said Darren.

"So either Lizzy or Tina weren't found," said Diana. "They might not even have died."

"I remember there was some speculation at the time. It was Lizzy who wasn't found. That's probably why I remember her so well," said Mildred. "But the house was completely destroyed. No one would have survived. The police, the military and the villagers spent a lot of time going through the rubble. It was a gruesome job. But they never found her."

There was a pause as everyone took this in.

"Ironically the Davies were a family of evacuees from London," continued Mildred. "They were bombed out there too."

"So the Davies could be the reason for the increased energy levels. More than just the normal thunder and lightning," said Diana.

"What we saw and heard and the story of the Davies aren't necessarily linked," said Art trying to be logical. But it was difficult not to make the connections.

"We have five independent witnesses," argued Diana. "And we all heard voices, including human voices. There was a trauma and there is an unanswered question. What happened to Lizzy? Maybe she wants to be found, to join the rest of her family. That's the unfinished business."

"It's a nice story," said Darren. "But really that's all it is. We have no idea what we are witnessing and why."

"OK," challenged Diana. "Say it's a hypothesis. What would prove or disprove it?"

"Finding a body?" suggested Joe.

"If we find could find Lizzy, give her proper burial. May be that would dissipate the energy," said Diana.

"Even that proves nothing," said Art. "OK we know that there is a missing child. The police reports and Mildred's account are the evidence for that. But say we found a body? Highly unlikely but say we did? That still doesn't give us a direct connection to what we saw and heard during last night's storm."

"It's a pretty big coincidence. We heard the soundtrack behind the Davies' story."

"You could be right," broke in Darren. "But even if you are we don't know that the discovery of Lizzy's remains will dissipate the signal. If the recording of that event is hardwired into the ground, then it will continue to replay under the same atmospheric conditions."

"So where do we go from here?" asked Diana. "If we can't make a connection. It's all just a bunch of coincidences."

"I'm afraid it usually is," said Darren. "At the end of the day everyone decides how they want to interpret the data and there are usually many ways. It's the magic and the frustration of this world."

"Except for Munch," said Joe slowly.

Munch was Joe's dog. A beautiful black and white collie.

"What's Munch got to do with this?" asked Art.

"Well Munch is always digging and barking around that area. Every time we go for a walk."

"So…?" said Darren.

"Well if we took a look at your readings and pinpointed the high energy areas perhaps we could get Munch to take a look."

"A sort of sniffer dog?" asked Diana

"Something like that," said Joe.

"But you've no scent to offer her," pointed out Mildred.

"In the absence of anything else, it's still worth a go," said Darren.

"Well let me know if you find anything," said Mildred getting to her feet. "It would be nice to say a proper goodbye if you did find Lizzy."

"I'm surprised that you think there is anything in this, Mildred," said Art. "I would have thought you were a non believer."

"When you've lived as long as I have," responded Mildred, "you will know that there are more things in the universe than anyone can comprehend and that nothing is impossible. For all you know even this very house - the Old Vicarage (that's a ridiculous name for a modern house, by the way) - may have powers of its own." She looked round the room and nodded.

Smart cookie, that Mildred.

* * * * * * * * *

The next day Diana was at work when the phone call came through. Art was in a rare state of excitement.

"It was exactly as Joe thought," he said. "We all went up to the site after breakfast with Munch. We took her to the points Darren identified as generating the most energy. She sniffed around for thirty minutes, wagging her tail and barking like she always does. Then, just as we were about to give up, she started to dig. After about fifteen seconds she unearthed a doll. Diana, imagine that. An old ragged doll. So we got a trowel and started to move some earth."

He gulped and there were tears in his voice.

"We found her, Diana. We found the child, Lizzy."

"Oh my goodness. So what's happening now?"

"We called the police. The area's cordoned off. But it can't be anything else."

* * * * * * * * *

Later that day they gathered together again: Joe, Mildred, Darren, Art and Diana. Their chatter was full of the events of the day but there were also a number of times when they fell silent, reflecting on the family, the tragedy of the bomb and their recent discovery.

Darren was leaving the next day. "How much extra do I owe you for all the hospitality?" he said.

Diana was quick to answer. "I don't think we can charge you now. At least not for the extra days. We've both come to think of you as a friend."

"You've certainly woken us all up," said Art. "With the magic mushrooms and now this."

"You won't make much money if you turn all your guests into friends," said Darren.

"So that's where we've been going wrong," laughed Art.

"What are you going to do next?" asked Diana.

"Well. I'm going to do some more research and then I'll write up my findings for our society's journal," said Darren.

"There is no doubt with five witnesses it will cause enormous excitement. And it could be very good news for you too."

"How so?" said Art.

"You may find that business becomes very brisk in a few months once word gets out," said Darren.

Diana and Art looked at each other.

"Looks like rumours of our demise may be exaggerated," said Art. "Minefield Old Vicarage B&B will live to fight another day."

Printed in Great Britain
by Amazon